Two Little Women

Carolyn Wells

Two Little Women

ISBN: 978-1-63637-842-8

CONTENTS

CHAPTER I   The Girl Next Door   1
CHAPTER II   Dotty Rose And Dolly Fayre   8
CHAPTER III   The New Rooms   15
CHAPTER IV   The Birthday Morning   22
CHAPTER V   The Double Party   29
CHAPTER VI   Roller Skating   36
CHAPTER VII   Two Big Brothers   44
CHAPTER VIII   Crosstrees Camp   52
CHAPTER IX   Dolly's Escape   59
CHAPTER X   Hidden Treasure   66
CHAPTER XI   A Thrilling Experience   74
CHAPTER XII   Who Was The Tall Phantom?   82
CHAPTER XIII   That Luncheon   91
CHAPTER XIV   The Cake Contest   99
CHAPTER XV   Who Won the Prize? 105
CHAPTER XVI   A Walk in the Woods 113
CHAPTER XVII   Surfwood 122
CHAPTER XVIII   Doll Overboard! 127
CHAPTER XIX   Spending The Prize Money 135
CHAPTER XX   Good-bye, Summer! 141

CHAPTER I

THE GIRL NEXT DOOR

Summit Avenue was the prettiest street in Berwick. Spacious and comfortable-looking homes stood on either side of it, each in its setting of lawn and shade trees. Most of these showed no dividing fences or hedges, and boundaries were indiscernible in the green velvety sward that swept in a gentle slope to the sidewalk.

Of two neighbouring houses, the side windows faced each other across two hundred feet of intervening turf. The windows of one house were duly fitted with window-screens, holland shades and clean, fresh white curtains; for it was May, and Berwick ladies were rarely dilatory with their "Spring-cleaning." But the other house showed no window dressings, and the sashes were flung open to the sunny breeze, which, entering, found rugless floors and pictureless walls.

But at the open front doors other things were entering; beds, chairs, tables, boxes and barrels, all the contents of the great moving vans that stood out at the curb. Strong men carried incredibly heavy burdens of furniture, or carefully manœuvred glass cabinets or potted palms.

From behind the lace curtains of the other house people were watching. This was in no way a breach of good manners, for in Berwick the unwritten law of neighbours' rights freely permitted the inspection of the arriving household gods of a new family. But etiquette demanded that the observers discreetly veil themselves behind the sheltering films of their own curtains.

And so the Fayres, mother and two daughters, watched with interest the coming of the Roses.

"Rose! what a funny name," commented Dolly Fayre, the younger of the sisters; "do you s'pose they name the children Moss, and Tea and things like that?"

"Yes, and Killarney and Sunburst and Prince Camille de Rohan," said Trudy, who had been studying Florists' catalogues of late.

"Their library furniture is mission; there goes the table," and Mrs. Fayre noted details with a housekeeper's eye. "And here comes the piano. I can't bear to see men move a piano; I always think it's going to fall on them."

"I'm tired of seeing furniture go in, anyway," and Dolly jumped

1

up from her kneeling position. "I'd rather see the people. Do you s'pose there's anybody 'bout my age, Mums?"

"I don't know, Dolly. Your father only said their name was Rose, and not another word about them."

"There's a little girl, anyway," asserted Trudy; "they took in a big doll's carriage some time ago."

Trudy was nineteen and Dolly not quite fifteen, so the girls, while chummy as sisters, had few interests in common. Dolly wandered away, leaving the other two to continue their appraisal of the new neighbours. She went to her own room, which also looked out toward the Roses' house. Idly glancing that way from her window, she saw a girl's face in a window next door. She seemed about Dolly's age, and she had a pretty bright face with a mop of curly black hair.

She wore a red dress and a red hair-ribbon, and she made a vivid picture, framed in the open window.

Dolly looked through the scrim of her bedroom curtain, and then to see better, moved the curtain aside, and watched the black-haired girl.

Dolly, herself, could not be seen, because of the dark wire window screen, and she looked at the stranger with increasing interest.

At last the new girl put one foot over the window sill and then the other, and sat with her feet crossed and kicking against the side of the house. It was a first floor window, and there was little danger of her falling out, but she stretched out her arms and held the window frame on either side.

Dolly judged the girl must be about her own age, for she looked so, and too, her dress came nearly but not quite to her shoetops, which was the prescribed length of Dolly's own.

It was a pleasant outlook. If this new neighbour should be a nice girl, Dolly foresaw lots of good times. For most of her girl friends lived at some distance; the nearest, several blocks away. And to have a chum next door would be fine!

But was she a nice girl? Dolly had been punctiliously brought up, and a girl who sat in a window, and swung her feet over the sill, was a bit unconventional in Berwick.

Dolly was seized with a strong desire to meet this girl, to see her nearer by and to talk with her. But Dolly was timid. Beside her careful education in deportment, she was naturally shy and reticent. She was sure she never could make any advances to become acquainted with this new girl, and yet, she did want to know her.

She went back to her mother and sister.

"There's an awful big picture," Trudy was saying; "it's all

burlapped up, so you can't tell what it is. It's easy to judge people from their pictures."

Trudy had graduated the year before from a large and fine girls' school and she knew all about pictures.

"I think you can tell more by chairs," Mrs. Fayre said; "their easy chairs are very good ones. I think they're very nice people."

"Have you seen the girl in the window?" asked Dolly. "She's just about my size."

"So she is," said Mrs. Fayre, glancing at Dolly, and then returning to her study of the chairs.

"When can I go to see her, Mother?"

"Oh, Trudy and I will call there in a fortnight or so, and after that you can go to see the little girl or I'll ask her mother to bring her over here. You children needn't be formal."

"But can't I go over there to-day?"

"Mercy, no, child! Not the day they arrive! They'd think we were crazy!"

Dolly went out on the side verandah. The black-haired girl still sat in the window. She was frankly staring, and so, every time Dolly caught her eye, the straightforward gaze was so disconcerting that Dolly looked away quickly and pretended to be engrossed in something else.

But at last with a determined effort to overcome her timidity, she concluded she would look over at the girl and smile. It couldn't be wrong merely to smile at a new girl, if it was the very day she arrived. They couldn't think her "crazy" for that. But to conclude to do this and to do it, were two very different matters for Dolly Fayre.

Half a dozen times she almost raised her eyes, her smile all ready to break out, and then, it would seem too much to dare, and with a deep blush, she would turn again toward her own house.

But it was nearing luncheon time, and Dolly made a last desperate effort to screw her courage to the sticking point. With a determined jerk she wheeled around and smiled broadly at the new girl.

To her amazement, the pretty face scowled at her! Definitely and distinctly scowled! Dolly could scarcely believe her eyes. Why should this stranger scowl at her, when she didn't know her at all?

Dolly quickly looked away, and pondered over the matter. She felt less shy now, because she was angry. Then the bell rang for luncheon.

Dolly started for the house, but unable to resist a final impulse, she glanced again at the girl in the window.

The girl shook her head at her! It was a quick, saucy, sideways shake, as if Dolly had asked her something and she had refused. The

3

pretty face looked pettish, and the black eyes snapped as she vigorously shook her curly head.

"Pooh!" said Dolly to herself; "wait till you're asked, miss! I don't want anything of you!"

Dolly went into the house and at the lunch table, she told her mother and Trudy of the girl's actions.

"I thought she looked saucy," said Trudy, and the subject was dropped.

In the meantime the girl next door had drawn in her feet and jumped down from the window.

"What a funny lunch!" she exclaimed, as she ran into the dining-room. "Looks good, though," and she sat down on a packing-box, and took the plate her mother offered.

"Yes, it's a sort of picnic," said Mrs. Rose; "everything's cold, but it does taste good!"

The dining-room was unfurnished; though the table and chairs were in it, they were still burlapped, and the barrels of dishes were not yet unpacked. Mrs. Rose and her sister, Mrs. Bayliss, sat on packing-boxes too, and made merry at their own discomfort.

"Seems 'sif we'd never get straightened out," said Mrs. Rose, taking another sandwich on her plate, "but I s'pose we will. It's always like this when you move. Thank goodness, George is coming home early,—he's such a help."

"Yes, he is," agreed Mrs. Bayliss; "what lovely fresh radishes! I'll take some more. Do you know any one at all in Berwick, Molly?"

"No one at all. George liked the place, and he bought this house from an agent. But I shan't hasten to make acquaintances. I believe in going slow in such matters. The neighbours will probably call after a few weeks, and then we'll see what they're like. The people next door have lovely curtains. I think you can judge a lot by curtains. And their whole place has a well-kept air. Perhaps they'll prove pleasant neighbours. Their name is Fayre."

"I saw the little girl out on the verandah," said Dotty Rose, between two bites of her sandwich. "She has yellow hair and blue eyes. But I don't like her."

"Why, Dotty, how you talk!" exclaimed her aunt; "how can you like her or dislike her, when you don't know her?"

"She's a prig; I can see that, Aunt Clara. I can tell by the way she walks and moves around. She hasn't any go to her."

"Well, you've go enough for the whole neighbourhood! Probably you'll find she's a nice, well-behaved little girl."

"All right, have it just as you like, Aunt Clara. When are you going to fix my room, Mother?"

4

"As soon as your things come; not till to-morrow, most likely. If we can get beds to sleep on to-night, that's all I'll ask."

"I think it's fun," and Dotty danced around on one toe; "I'd like to live this way, always,—nothing in its place and all higgledy-piggledy!"

"I believe you would," returned her mother, laughing. "Now, if you've finished your lunch, dearie, run away and play, for you only bother around here."

Dotty ran away but she didn't play. She went from one room to another, trying to learn the details of her new home; but ever and anon her glance would stray to the house next door, and she would wonder what the yellow-haired girl was doing.

Dotty had been allowed to choose her own room from two that her mother designated. One was on the side of the house that faced the Fayres', the other wasn't. Dotty hesitated between them. She went in one and then the other.

"If I should like that prim-faced thing," she said to her Aunt Clara, "I'd rather have this room, that looks toward their house. But if I don't like her,—and I'm just about sure I won't,—I'd rather have my room on the other side."

"Oh, you'll like her, after you know her," said Aunt Clara, carelessly. "But don't mind that, take the room you think pleasanter."

So Dotty considered them both again. The room not facing the Fayres' was without doubt the more attractive of the two, though not much so. It had a large bay window, which was delightful; but then on the other hand the other room had an open fireplace, and Dotty loved a wood fire.

She stood in the room with the fireplace, looking toward the next house. It was Saturday afternoon, and as she watched she saw the yellow-haired girl and two ladies come out and get in a motor car.

"I don't like her!" Dotty declared again, though as there was no one else present, she talked to herself. "She walks like a prig, she gets in the car like a prig and she sits down on the seat like a prig! I don't like her, and I'm going to take the other room!"

So, when her own furniture arrived it was put in the room with the bay window and which did not overlook the Fayre house. The house that she could see from her newly chosen room, was so hemmed in by trees as to be almost invisible.

Dotty spent a pleasant afternoon, after her furniture was in place, arranging her little trinkets and pictures, and putting away things in her cupboards and bureau drawers.

But every little while some errand seemed to call her across the

5

hall, and she couldn't help looking out to see if "that girl" had returned yet.

The next day was Sunday, and Mr. Rose was at home.

"Well, Chick-a-dotty, you'll have a nice playmate in that little girl next door," he said, as his daughter followed him round the house looking after various matters.

"'Deed I won't, Daddy; she's horrid!"

"Why, why! what sort of talk is this? Do you know her?"

"No, but I've seen her, and she isn't nice a bit."

"Oh, I guess she is. I came out in the train last night with a man I know, and he knows the Fayres and he says they're about the nicest people in Berwick."

"Pooh! I don't think so. She's a prim old thing, and doesn't know B from broomstick."

"There, there, Dotty Doodle, don't be hasty in your judgment. Give the little lady a chance."

Later, Dotty and her father walked round the outdoors part of their new domain.

"Isn't it pretty, Daddy!" exclaimed Dotty; "I'm so glad there are a lot of flower-beds and nice big shrubs, and lovely blue spruce trees and lots of things that look like a farm."

The Roses had always lived in the city, and to Dotty's eyes the two acres of ground seemed like a large estate. It was attractively laid out and in good cultivation, and Mr. Rose looked forward with pleasure to the restful life of a suburban town after his city habits.

"There's that girl now!" and Dotty suddenly spied her neighbour walking with her father around their lawn.

"So it is. I shall speak to him; it's only right, as we are next-door neighbours, and we men needn't be so formal as the ladies of the houses."

"I don't want to speak to her," and Dotty drew back. "Don't do it, Daddy, please don't!"

"Nonsense, child! of course I shall. Don't be so foolish."

"But I don't want to; she'll think I'm crazy to meet her, and I'm not! I don't want to, Father."

"What a silly! Well, if you don't want to see the girl now, run away. I'm certainly going to chat with Mr. Fayre, and get acquainted."

Now the other pair of neighbours had, not unnaturally, been talking about the newcomers.

"You see, Father," said Dolly as she took her usual Sunday morning stroll around the place with him, "that new girl isn't nice at all. When I smiled at her, she scowled and shook her head at me."

"Oh, Dolly, I imagine she's all right. Mr. Forrest told me about them. He knows them and he says they're charming people."

"Well, they may be, but I don't want to meet her. Don't walk over that way."

"Yes, I shall. Mr. Rose seems to be coming this way, and I shall do the neighbourly thing and have a chat with him."

"Why, Father, you don't know him."

"That doesn't matter between next-door neighbours, at least between the men of the houses. Come along, and scrape acquaintance with the little girl. I think she looks pretty."

Dolly started, then a sudden fit of shyness seized her, and she stood stock-still.

"I can't," she murmured; "oh, Father, please don't ask me to!"

"All right, dear; don't if you don't want to. Run back to the house. I'm going to speak to Mr. Rose."

And that's how it happened that as the two men neared each other, with greeting smiles, the two girls, started simultaneously, and ran like frightened rabbits away from each other, and to their respective homes.

CHAPTER II

DOTTY ROSE AND DOLLY FAYRE

A few days passed without communication between the two houses.

Mr. Fayre expressed a decided approval of his new neighbour, and advised his wife to call on Mrs. Rose. Mrs. Fayre said she would do so as soon as the proper time came.

"I'm not going," said Dolly. "I don't like that girl, and I never shall."

"Why, Dorinda," said her father, who only used her full name when he was serious, "I've never known you to act so before. I've thought you were a nice, sweet-tempered little girl, and here you are acting like a cantankerous catamaran!"

"What is the matter with you, Doll?" asked Trudy; "you are unreasonable about the little Rose girl."

"Let her alone," said Dolly's mother; "she'll get over it."

"I'll never get over it," declared Dolly; "I don't want to know a girl as big as I am, who plays with dolls."

"How do you know she plays with dolls?"

"Well, a dolls' carriage went in there the day they moved in."

"Perhaps it's one she used to have, and she has kept it, for old associations."

"Maybe. Anyhow, I don't like her. She made faces at me."

"Really?" and her mother smiled.

"Well, she scowled at me, and shook her head like a—like a—"

"Like a little girl shaking her head," said Mr. Fayre, to help her out.

But Dolly didn't smile. She was a queer nature, was Dolly. Usually sunny and happy-hearted, she liked almost everything and everybody, but if she did take a dislike, it became a prejudice, and very hard to remove.

Dolly was pretty, with the bluest of blue eyes and the pinkest of pink cheeks and the yellowest of yellow hair. She was inclined to be plump, and Trudy was always beseeching her not to eat so much candy and sweet desserts. But Dolly loved these things and had small concern about her increasing weight. She didn't care much for outdoor play, and would rather sit in the hammock and read a story-book than run after tennis balls.

Her mother called her a dreamer, and often came upon her, sitting in the twilight, her thoughts far away in a fairyland of her

8

own imagination, enjoying wonderful adventures and thrilling scenes.

Dolly was in the grammar school and next year would be in the high school. She didn't like study, particularly, except history and literature, but she studied conscientiously and always knew her lessons.

This morning, she kissed her mother good-bye, and started off for school. She wore a blue and white gingham, and a fawn-coloured coat. Swinging her bag of books, she marched past the Rose house, and though she didn't look at her, she could see the Rose girl on the front steps.

"I wonder if she'll go to our school," thought Dolly; and for a moment the impulse seized her to stop and "scrape acquaintance." Then she remembered that shaking head, and fearing a rebuff, she walked on by.

"Do you know that new girl next door to you?" Celia Ferris asked her as she entered the school yard.

"No; do you?" and Dolly looked indifferent.

"No, I don't; but my mother knows a lady, who knows them and she says Dorothy,—that's her name,—is a wonder."

"A wonder! How?"

"Oh, she's so smart and so clever, and she can do everything so well."

This was enough for Dolly Fayre. To think that disagreeable new neighbour of hers, must be a paragon of all the virtues!

But Dolly was never unjust. She knew she had no real reason to dislike Dorothy Rose, so she only said, "I haven't met her yet. My mother is going to call there this week, and then I s'pose I'll get acquainted with her."

"How funny," said Celia, who was chummy by nature. "I should think you'd go in and play with her without waiting for your mother to call,—and all that. Anybody'd think you were as old as Trudy."

"Oh, I could do that if I wanted to, but I don't want to."

"Well, I think I'll go to see her, anyway. If she's so smart it would be nice to have her in the Closing Day exercises. I s'pose she'll come to school here."

"Of course, you can do as you like, Celia, but I think it's too late to get any new girls in now."

Dolly went on to the schoolroom, her heart full of resentment at this "smart" interloper. It was a little bit a feeling of jealousy, for Dolly Fayre was head and front of everything that went on at the Berwick Grammar School, and it jarred a little to think of having a wonder-girl come in with a lot of new ideas and plans and mix everything all up at the last minute.

9

But don't get any mistaken idea that Dolly Fayre was a mean-minded or small-natured girl. On the contrary, she was generosity itself in all her dealings with her schoolmates. Every one liked her, and with good reason, for she never quarrelled, and was always happy and smiling.

But the Rose girl had acted queer from the first, and Dolly couldn't admit the desirability of bringing her into their already arranged "Closing Exercises." These were so important as to be almost sacred rites, and as usual Dolly was at the head of all the committees, and her word was law.

She went home from school that afternoon, thinking about it, and her pretty face looked very sober as she went in the house and put her school-books neatly away in their place.

"There's some lemonade and cookies on the sideboard," said her mother as Dolly went through the hall.

"All right, Mumsie," and somehow, after these refreshments had been absorbed, Dolly felt better, and life seemed to have a brighter outlook.

She took an unfinished story-book and picked up her white kitten, and went out to the side verandah, her favourite spot of a warm afternoon.

"You see, Flossy," she whispered, addressing the kitten, "I want you with me, 'cause I'm buffled to-day." Dolly was in the habit of making up words, if she couldn't think of any to suit her, and just at the moment buffled seemed to her to mean a general state of being ruffled, and buffeted and rebuffed and generally huffy.

"And you well know, Floss, that when I feel mixy-up, there's nothing so comforting and soothing as a nice little, soft little, cuddly little kitty-cat."

Flossy blinked her eyes, and purred gently, and was just as comforting as she could be, which is saying a good deal.

There was a big, wide swing on the side verandah, one of those cushioned settee affairs that are so cosy to snuggle into, and read.

And it was without a glance at the house next door, that Dolly snuggled herself in among the red cushions and opened her book, while Flossy cuddled in the hollow of her arm; and concluding that she would be quite as comforting asleep as awake, the kitten promptly fell into a doze.

Meantime there were arrivals at the Rose house.

Eugenia, the eleven year old girl, had been staying with a cousin until the house should be put in order, and now she had come to the new home.

She was a black-haired witch, and of exceeding vivacious and volatile disposition.

10

"OO!—ee!" she exclaimed; "isn't it great! Take me everywhere, Dot! Show me all the rooms and all the outdoorses and everything! I didn't know it was such a big house. Which is my room?"

Even as she talked, Eugenia was flying upstairs, only to turn right around and fly down again. She danced from room to room, sometimes followed or preceded by Dotty and sometimes not. Her own room delighted her. It faced the Fayres' house, being the one Dorothy had rejected in favour of the other.

"Where's Blot?" asked Dotty; "didn't you bring him?"

"Oh, yes; he's down with Thomas. He's crazy. He barked all the way here."

But Dotty was already flying down stairs to find her beloved puppy.

"Here he is, Miss Dorothy," and the chauffeur, Thomas, gave the black poodle into her arms.

"Oh, you blessed Blotty-boy! Oh, you cunnin' Blotsy-wotsy! Does him love hims Dotty?"

The love was manifested by some moist caresses and then Blot was all for a scamper. Dotty took him out on the lawn and set him down, herself all ready for a romp.

Now only a minute before, Flossy, the white kitten, had waked from her nap, and seeing that Dolly was absorbed in her story-book, inferred that kitten comfort was not at the moment needed, and decided to go after a very yellow butterfly out on the Fayre lawn.

Stealthily across the grass, Flossy went butterflywards, on tippy-toe. Each white paw was daintily lifted and softly set down on the thick turf, as her progress continued. From the Rose lawn Blot spied the advancing Flossy. He didn't then know her name, but he had liberal ideas on the subject of introductions, and he made a wild dash toward the oncoming kitten.

When Floss saw the small black whirlwind hurling itself at her, she was either too brave or too frightened to retreat, so she put her white back up as high as possible and stood her ground. She expressed her opinion of the performance in a series of sputtering yowls that drew Dolly's attention from her book to the impending battle.

She sprang out of the swing, and rushed toward Flossy just as the two belligerents met in the grassy arena.

Dorothy Rose, on her side of the lawn was shaking with laughter, and this sight was the last straw to Dorinda Fayre's overburdened soul.

"Don't you let your dog eat up my cat!" she cried out, angrily, to the black-haired girl opposite.

"Don't you let your cat eat up my dog, then!" was the immediate response, delivered with enthusiasm equalling Dolly's own.

"Cats don't eat dogs!"

"Neither do dogs eat cats!"

"Well, these will eat each other! Oh! look, we must get them apart!"

The battle was of the pitched variety, whatever that may mean. But it is a phrase used to describe the most intense and desperate battles of history, and surely this was one of them. Dolly Fayre had no idea that gentle little Flossy had so much fight in her small white body, and Dotty Rose never dreamed that Blot was such a fire-eater under his curly black coat.

Really alarmed for their pets, the two girls went nearer to the agile warriors, who now looked like an indistinct moving-picture film that was going too fast.

"Come here, Blot!" Dotty cried, in most commanding tones.

"Come here, Flossy!" Dolly called, in coaxing accents.

Insubordination ensued on both sides.

"We'll have to grab them!" declared Dotty Rose; dancing about the war zone.

"We can't!" wailed Dolly Fayre, wringing her hands as she edged away from the seat of battle.

"Well, I just guess we will!" and Dotty Rose seized Blot by the scruff of his black neck and shook him loose from the white kitten.

With a little cry of rejoicing, Dolly Fayre picked up Flossy and plumped herself down on the grass to make sure the kitten was intact.

Dotty sat down too, and felt of Blot's small and well-hidden bones.

As neither animal gave any cry of pain and as each glared at its late opponent, the respective owners of the combatants drew sighs of relief and held on tightly to their pets, lest a fresh attack should begin.

Now it stands to reason that after a scene like that just described, the two girls couldn't get up and walk off home without a word.

So they sat on the grass and looked at each other.

And when the troubled blue eyes of Dolly Fayre saw the big brown eyes of Dotty Rose twinkle and saw her red lips smile, she discovered that the scowl she had objected to was not permanent, and she smiled back.

But somehow, they could think of nothing to say. The smile broke the ice a little, but Dolly Fayre was timid, and Dotty Rose was absorbed in looking at the other's blue eyes and yellow hair.

12

But it was Dotty who spoke first. "Well," she said, "how do you like me?"

It was an unfortunate question. For Dolly Fayre hadn't a single definite notion regarding Dotty Rose except that she didn't like her. However, it would hardly do to tell her that, so she said, slowly: "I don't know yet; how do you like me?"

"Well, I think you're awfully pretty, to begin with."

"So do I you," put in Dolly, glad to find a favourable report that she could make truthfully.

"Aren't we different," went on the other thoughtfully; "you're so blonde and I'm so dark."

"Yes; I just hate my hair,—towhead, Bert calls me."

"Who's Bert?"

"He's my brother; he's away at school. He's seventeen years old." Dolly spoke proudly, as if she had said, "he's captain of the Fleet."

"Why, I've got a brother away at school, too."

"Have you? What's his name?"

"Bob; of course it's Robert, but we always call him Bob. He's eighteen."

"What else have you got?"

Dotty knew the question referred to family connections, and answered: "A little sister, Genie, 'leven years old."

"That all?"

"Yep. 'Cept Aunt Clara, who lives with us, she's a widow. And of course, Mother and Dad."

"I've got a grown-up sister, Trudy. She's in s'ciety now, and she's awful pretty."

"Look like you?"

"Some. But she's all fluffy-haired and dimply-smiled, you know."

"What funny words you use."

"Do I? Well, I only do when I can't think of the real ones. Are you going to the Grammar School?"

"Mother says it's too late to begin this year. Here it is May,— and it closes in June. So she says for me to wait till next year."

This was comforting. If the girl didn't go to school this year she couldn't make any bother with the Closing Exercises. Beside, maybe she was not such a dislikable girl as she had seemed at first. Dolly sat and regarded her. At last she said: "Then the doll-carriage belongs to your little sister."

"To Genie, yes. How did you know she had one?"

"Saw it come with your things, the day you moved in."

"How old are you?"

13

"Fourteen, but I'll be fifteen next month,—June."

"Why, so will I! Isn't that funny! What day is your birthday?"

"The tenth."

"Mine's the twentieth. We're almost twins. And our names are quite alike, too. Mine's Dorothy, really, but they all call me Dotty."

"And mine's Dorinda, but I'm called Dolly."

"And we both have brothers at school, and we each have a sister."

"But mine is a big sister and yours is a little sister."

"Yes, but we have as many differences as we have likenesses. You're so fair, and—why, your name is Fayre!"

Dolly laughed. "Yes, and you're so rosy and your name is Rose!"

"Dotty Rose and Dolly Fayre! We ought to be friends. Shall we?"

Dolly hesitated. She was too honest to pretend to a liking she didn't quite feel. She looked squarely at Dotty Rose, and said, straightforwardly, "What made you scowl at me that first day you came?"

"I didn't!" and Dotty Rose opened her brown eyes in astonishment.

"Yes, you did; and you shook your head at me when I smiled to you. You were sitting in a window, with your legs hanging out."

"Sitting where! Oh, I remember! Why, I didn't scowl at you, it was because Aunt Clara called me to come in out of that window. And I didn't want to, so I scowled. I've a fearful temper. And then, she told me again to come in, and I shook my head. I wasn't shaking it at you! Why, I didn't know you then!"

Dolly drew a long breath. "Then that's all right! I thought you scowled because I smiled at you, and it made me mad. All right, I'll be friends with you. I'd like to. I think you're real nice."

"So do I you!"

CHAPTER III

THE NEW ROOMS

In the cushioned swing on the Fayres' verandah the two girls sat.

An artist would have stopped to admire the picture. Dorinda, her pink and white face framed in its golden halo of curlilocks, her light blue frock, neat and smooth, was calmly and daintily nibbling at a piece of cake, catching the crumbs carefully as they fell.

Beside her, Dorothy was rapidly munching her cake as she talked, and letting the crumbs fall where they might. Her black hair framed her rosy cheeks and her eyes snapped and sparkled as she gesticulated with both hands. It was Dorothy's habit to emphasise her remarks with expressive little motions, and her father often said that if her hands were tied behind her, she couldn't say a word!

Her pink lawn dress was rather tumbled by reason of her wriggling and jumping about, but Dorothy's frocks were rarely unrumpled after she had had them on ten minutes.

"We've been friends more than a week now," she said, as she finished her cake in one large bite and brushed a few stray bits out of her lap. "And I think you're just fine! I'm so glad we came to live in Berwick. I like you better than any girl I ever knew." Dotty spread her hands wide as if embracing all the girls who had figured in her previous existence. "Do you like me as much as that?"

As she spoke, she touched her toes to the floor and sent the swing up in the air with a mad jump.

"Oh!" gasped Dolly, as her cake flew out of her hand; "how—how sudden you are!"

"Never mind! Do you like me as much as I like you?"

"I don't know," and Dolly looked thoughtful; "I like you, of course, but I wish you'd sit stiller."

"Can't; I'm always jumpy. But you do like me, don't you, Dollyrinda?"

"Yes, but I can't hop into a liking the way you do. We're awfully different, you know."

"'Course we are! That's what makes us like each other. Just think, Dolly, we'll be fifteen soon. Don't you think we ought to be called by our full names and not Dolly and Dotty any more?"

"I don't know. Why?"

"Oh, 'cause we're too big for baby names. I'm going to stop wearing hair-ribbons."

15

"You are! How ever will you keep your hair back? And you've such a lot of it."

"I know. So've you. Why, I'll just braid it, and let the end flutter. But Mother says she won't let me till I'm sixteen. Well, we'll see. Do you want to grow up, Doll?"

"I don't know."

"You don't know anything! I never saw such a girl! Well, what are you going to do when you're fifteen?"

"I haven't thought about it. Do I have to do anything different from when I'm fourteen?"

"You don't have to! But don't you want to? What do you want to be when you're grown up?"

"Oh, then! Why, then I'm going to be an opera singer."

"Can you sing?"

"Not much yet. But Trudy says I have a nice voice and I'm going to learn."

"Pooh! I don't believe you'll ever sing in opera. I'm going to be an actress."

"Huh! Can you act?"

"Not yet; but I'm going to learn." Dotty smiled as she realised that their ambitions were at least equally promising. "Wouldn't it be fun if we did both get to be famous! Me an actress and you a singeress. But I may change my mind about mine. I do sometimes. Last winter I was crazy to be a trained nurse; but Mother wouldn't let me."

"Will she let you be an actress?"

"I haven't asked her yet. There's no hurry. I couldn't begin to study for it till I'm out of school. What are you going to get for your birthday?"

"I haven't decided yet. Mother said I could have my bedroom all done over or have a gold watch."

"Oh, have the room things. And I'll do the same! Do you know, when we moved into our house, I took a room on the other side, but I'm going to move across so I can be on this side toward you. And Mother is going to have the room done up for me, and I'm to choose the things. So you do that too, and we'll have 'em alike!"

Dotty had jumped out of the swing in her excitement, and stood at one side, her foot on the step, pushing it sideways.

"Don't do that, Dot, you'll break the swing."

"Well, will you? Will you choose the room fixings 'stead of the watch?"

"I don't know; I'll have to think."

"Fiddlesticks! Don't think! Jump at it, and say yes!"

"I believe I'd rather, anyway; it would be fun to have our things alike. I'll ask Mother."

"But she said you could have your choice."

"Yes, but of course, I'll talk it over with her. And Dotty, we don't want the same coloured things, you know."

"Why don't we?"

"Why, because we're so different. What colour do you want?"

"Oh, I've got it all picked out. I'm going to have rose and grey. It's all the rage. Rose pink, you know, and French grey."

"Well, I don't want that. I want pale green and white."

"You do! Why rose and grey is ever so much more fashionable."

"I don't care. I know what I want. Now, see here,— But do come and sit down! Don't climb over the back of the swing!"

Dotty jumped down from the back of the swing, and came around and seated herself beside Dolly. For nearly five minutes she sat quietly while they discussed the colours.

"But, don't you see," said Dolly at last, "it will be nicer for us to have our own colours and have the things alike. We can have just the same shape furniture and everything, only each stick to our own colour."

Dotty was persuaded, and they agreed that the two mothers could easily be brought to see the beauty of their plans.

And so it was. A neighbourly friendliness already existed between the households, and as the two birthdays fell so near together, it seemed fitting that the girls should have their gifts alike.

So the paperhanger was visited and Dolly chose a lovely paper of striped pattern, but all white; to be crowned with a border design of hanging vines and leaves in shades of green.

Dotty's paper was the same stripe, in soft greys; and her border was a design of pink roses and rosebuds.

Dolly's woodwork was to be painted white and Dotty's light grey.

The two sets of furniture were exactly alike, except that one was enamelled grey and one white.

Each room had a bay window, and the window seats were cushioned in green or rose, and the numerous pillows that graced them were of harmonious colouring.

The parents of the girls agreed that a fifteenth birthday was a memorable occasion, and one not likely to occur again, so they made the furnishings of the two rooms complete to the smallest detail.

Each had a large rug of plain velvet carpeting; Dotty's rose pink and Dolly's moss green. Window curtains of Rajah silk fell over

17

dainty white ones, and pretty light-shades of green and pink, respectively, gave the rooms a soft glow at night.

Trudy contributed wonderful filet embroidered covers for dressing-tables and stands, and dainty white couch pillows, with monograms and ruffles.

Dotty's Aunt Clara gave each of the girls a picture, which they were allowed to choose for themselves. They took a whole afternoon for this, and at last Dolly made up her mind to take "Sir Galahad," and Dotty chose, after long deliberation, a stunning photograph of the "Winged Victory."

These, framed alike in dark, polished wood, were hung in similar positions in the two rooms.

Altogether, the rooms were delightful. It was hard to say which was prettier, but each best suited its happy owner.

There was quite a discussion as to when they would take possession, for everything was in readiness by Dolly's birthday, which was on the tenth.

"I'll tell you!" cried Dotty, with a sudden inspiration; "let's average up! Dolly's birthday is the tenth and mine the twentieth. Let's celebrate both on the fifteenth, that's half way between, and as we're fifteen anyway, it makes it just right!"

This was agreed to as a fine scheme, and then Mrs. Fayre electrified the girls by proposing that they have a little party by way of further celebration.

"Together, of course," she said, smiling; "not in either house, but an outdoor party, on the lawn, half-way between."

"Oh, Mumsie!" and Dolly clasped her hands in ecstatic joy at the prospect.

"Oh, Mrs. Fayre!" and Dotty flung her hands above her head, and danced up and down the room where these plans were being talked over.

They were in the Fayre house, having just come down from an inspection of Dolly's room, and these inspections were of almost daily occurrence and usually participated in by several members of both families.

"Good idea!" said Mrs. Rose. "It will let Dotty get acquainted with the young people here, and that's what I want. But let me make the party, Mrs. Fayre, and you and Dolly invite the guests as we know so few people as yet."

"No; the party must be half and half as to responsibility and expense. If our two D's are to be so friendly, we must share and share alike in their doings."

So it was agreed, and as there was but a week in which to get ready, plans were hurried through.

18

They decided to ask thirty of the Berwick young people, fifteen girls and fifteen boys.

"I wish Bob could be home!" sighed Dotty; and Dolly echoed the wish for her own brother. But the boys of the two families were deep in school exams and could not think of coming home for a party.

Of course the Fayres decided on the invitation list, but everything else was mutually arranged.

It was to be entirely a lawn party; first because that seemed pleasanter, and too, because then, it could take place on the adjoining lawns and so be the party of both.

"Only,—if it rains!" said Dolly, with an anxious face.

"It won't rain!" declared Dotty; "it can't rain on our double birthday! It will be the beautifullest, clearest, sunshiniest day in the world! I know it will!"

The girls decided to sleep in their new rooms for the first time the night before the party.

"For," said Dolly, shaking her head sagely, "the night after the party, we'll be so tired and thinky about it, that we can't enjoy our rooms so much."

"All right," agreed Dotty, "I don't care. I'm crazy to get into mine; the sooner the better, I say."

The two girls had a birthday present for each other, and though they didn't know it, the two mothers had planned these so they should be alike.

But they did know that the mothers had these gifts in readiness, and that they would see them when they awoke on the birthday morning.

By common consent the real birthdays were ignored, and the fifteenth of June accepted as the right anniversary for both.

Very formal were the rites preparatory to the occupancy of the new rooms.

Dotty had planned them and after some discussion Dolly had agreed.

"You come over and wish me good-night in my room," Dotty said, "and then I'll go over and wish you good-night in yours. And then, I'll go home again, and when we're all ready for bed, we'll put out our lights and stick our heads out of our windows and holler good-night across."

"Somebody might hear us," objected Dolly.

"Pooh! they won't. And what if they did? Neighbours have got a right to say good-night to each other, I guess."

"But that's disturbing the peace, or something like that."

19

"Huh! the Peace must be awful easy disturbed! Well, you've got to do it, anyhow."

"I haven't got to, either! Not just 'cause you say so!"

Dotty was beginning to learn that mild-mannered Dolly had a will of her own, and she said, placatingly: "Well, what do you want to do, then?"

"Let's do something like this. When we're all ready to hop into bed, let's turn our lights up and down three times in succession; that'll mean good-night."

"Oh, yes, I see; now, listen! we'll do it separately. You flash first and then I will; and after three flashes, we'll leave the lights out and jump into bed at the same minute!"

So it was settled, and the eventful occasion duly arrived.

The girls' bedtime hour was nine o'clock, but some time before that they were in their new rooms, enjoying their beauty and freshness.

At quarter before nine, Dolly appeared at the Rose house, and said solemnly, "I've come over to wish Dorothy good-night."

"Come in," said Mrs. Rose, trying not to smile at the ceremonial visit. "You'll find her in her room; go right up."

Dolly went up, and found Dotty waiting for her.

"Isn't it pretty!" Dolly exclaimed, seeing, as if for the first time the beauties of the room. The bed was turned down, and a lovely new nightdress, with a rose-coloured ribbon run through its lace edge, lay in readiness for the sleeper.

"Oh, it's lovely!" returned Dotty; "I can hardly wait to go to bed! Go on, say your piece."

Dolly stood a minute, her hands clasped, her eyes wandering about with a thoughtful far away gaze.

"It's all gone," she said at last; "I can't remember it, only a line:

"Sleep sweetly in this quiet room, oh, thou, whoe'er
thou art;
Nor let a troublous something or other disturb thy
peaceful heart.

"Honest, that's all I can remember."

"Well, that's enough. Thank you, sweet friend and playmate, now go I with thee!"

Grabbing Dolly by the arm, Dotty flew downstairs and across the lawn to the other house; Dolly running by her side.

Up to Dolly's new room they went.

"Lovely!" exclaimed Dotty, as she saw almost the counterpart of

20

her own room, even to the new nightdress,—only Dolly's had a white ribbon.

"You might have had green," said Dotty, doubtfully.

"No, I don't like coloured ribbons in my underclothes. They're all right for you," Dolly added politely, "but I never did like them."

"Now I'll say my piece;" and Dotty bowed to her audience of one. "I haven't forgotten it, but it's very short.

"Early to bed and early to rise
Makes a girl healthy and wealthy and wise.

"Thank you, sweet friend and playmate, now go I with thee."

"No; you don't say that! You've been with me. Now, I go home and we both get ready for bed. When you're all ready, put out your light and—"

"Yes, I know."

Dotty scampered downstairs and over home, and fairly flew up to her room.

In less than twenty minutes Dotty was all ready for bed; she put out her light, and throwing a dressing-gown over her nightdress, she sat in the window, watching the light in Dolly's room.

She waited and waited, but the light behind the pulled-down shade remained.

"H'm!" said Dotty to herself, yawning, "she is the slowest thing! I could have undressed twice in this time!"

But at last, Dolly's light went out, and her shade was slowly raised.

Then, according to their plan, Dotty flashed her light on and off again. Dolly's light repeated this manœuvre. Then Dotty did it again, and then Dolly did. The third time the flashes came and went, and then all ceremonies over, the two girls went to their new pretty, inviting beds, and were very soon asleep.

CHAPTER IV

THE BIRTHDAY MORNING

Dotty Rose woke early next morning, and, wide-awake on the instant, sprang from her bed and flew to the window. But she could see nothing of Dolly. The white shades were down and there was no sign of any one stirring. Dotty turned back and began anew to look at her pretty belongings. On the dressing-table she spied something she had not seen there the night before. It was a lovely picture of Dolly in a beautiful silver frame. Dotty laughed outright, for that was exactly what she had given Dolly! A silver frame with her own picture in it. The two mothers had been in the secret, and had seen to it that the frames were alike, but neither of the girls knew that her gift was to be duplicated.

It was a perfect likeness, showing Dolly at her best; a dreamy expression on her sweet face, and her soft hair in little waves at her temples, and drawn back by an enormous ribbon bow.

It was almost too early to get dressed, so Dotty slipped on a dressing-gown and bedroom slippers and dawdled about, keeping a watch on the Fayre house, in hopes Dolly's shades would fly up.

Soon her little sister Eugenia came bounding in. She, too, was in a kimono and she gave a jump and landed with a spring in the middle of Dotty's carefully arranged couch pillows.

"Genie!" cried her sister, "get off of there!"

"Won't!" and Genie bounced up and down on the springs of the couch.

"Get off, I tell you!"

"Won't, I tell you!"

It was trying, for the pretty pillows with their snowy white embroidered covers were rumpled and tossed by Genie's mischievous play.

"Genie Rose! You go right straight out of my room! You're a naughty little girl and you're spoiling my birthday things!"

"Dorothy Rose,
With a pug nose!"

chanted Genie, with the amiable intention of teasing her sister beyond endurance.

And she did, for Dotty flung back:

22

and then she grabbed her and pulled her off the pillows and pushed her out of the room and locked the door.

"It's a shame!" and poor Dotty nearly cried to see the havoc naughty little Genie had wrought. One pillow cover was torn and another had a black mark from the sole of Genie's slipper.

She heard a tap at the door, and her mother's voice said, "Let me in, Dotty, dear."

Dotty opened the door, and exclaimed: "Mother! Isn't Genie the bad little thing! Look at my pretty pillows!"

"Oh, what a shame! Why do you two children quarrel so?"

"We didn't quarrel. Genie did it on purpose."

"But why can't you be loving, kind little sisters? You're always teasing each other."

"But I didn't tease her, Mother."

"Well, you usually do. Now, Dotty, can't you make a birthday resolution to be more patient with Genie? Remember she's only a little girl, while you're getting grown up. Fifteen is almost a young lady, and you should be kind and gentle with everybody."

"I s'pose I ought," and Dorothy sighed; "but it's hard to have my birthday things upset. Aren't you going to punish her, Mother?"

"Oh, no; she didn't mean to be naughty. She was only mischievous. I'll mend your pillow, and the soiled one can be laundered."

Dotty's anger was always quick to come and quick to go, and she smiled brightly, as she said, "all right. I'll forgive her this time, but she's got to stop that kind of teasing."

"I'll speak to her," said easy-going Mrs. Rose; "how do you like Dolly's picture?"

"Lovely, isn't it? Did you and Mrs. Fayre know about the frames?"

"Yes; and we wanted them to be alike; but I had to urge you to take this instead of that other pattern. Remember?"

"Yes, indeed," and Dotty smiled to think how determined she had been in the matter, but had at last yielded to her mother's judgment.

"Oh, there's Dolly!" she cried, as she saw the shade go up in the opposite window. "Hello. Happy Birthday!" she called out.

Dolly returned the greeting, and the two girls waved their respective photographs at each other, and then both began to get dressed.

Dolly, too, had a morning visit from her sister.

Trudy looked in on her way down to breakfast.

"Happy Birthday, Doll!" she said; "shall I tie your hair-ribbon?"

She stepped into the new room, and while tying the big bow, looked around admiringly.

"You're a lucky little kiddy to have such a lovely room. It's prettier than mine."

"I know it is, Trudy," and Dolly looked regretful. "I'll change with you, if you like. I think as you're the oldest you ought to have the prettiest room."

"Not at all, you little goosy!" and Trudy kissed the troubled face. "This is your fifteenth birthday, and I'm glad you have such a beautiful gift to remember it by."

With their arms around each other, the two girls went downstairs.

"Whoop-de-doo! Dollykins," cried her father, throwing down his paper; "why, you don't look a bit different from when you were fourteen! I thought you'd be a foot taller, at least!"

"I don't feel any taller or any older, Father; and I don't s'pose I'll act so. But Mumsie, mayn't I stop wearing hair-ribbons? Dotty's going to."

"Are you sure?" and Mrs. Fayre looked quizzical, for she had discussed this weighty matter with Mrs. Rose.

"No, not sure; but Dotty's going to ask her mother and she thinks she can make her say yes."

"Well, let's wait and see what Mrs. Rose does say," and Mrs. Fayre took her place at the breakfast table.

"It seems funny not to have a lot of presents at your place, Doll," said Trudy, smiling.

"That's all right," and Dolly returned the smile; "I agreed that my room fixings were to take the place of all other presents."

"And then you have the party, you know," said her father. "Mr. Rose has a delightful surprise for it, and when I come home this afternoon I'll bring something to add to the gaiety of nations."

"Oh, Father, what?"

"Never you mind, curiosity-box! You'll see soon enough."

"Will you come home early, Father?"

"As early as I can. By five, surely."

After breakfast, the two heroines of the occasion went out to their respective side verandahs, and the usual morning programme was carried out.

Each frantically waved her hand to the other, calling, "Come over!"

Then each vigorously shook her head, shouting: "No, you come over here!"

24

"No, you!"

"No, you!"

Then Dolly, coaxingly, "Aw, come on,—come on over."

Then Dotty, positively, "No, sir! it's your turn. Come on over here."

With slight variations this dialogue was repeated every morning. Not that either cared much which went to the other's house, but it was one of their habits. Perhaps Dolly oftenest gave in, and on this birthday morning, the colloquy was short before she ran across the grass and the two friends sat in the Roses' hammock, swinging vigorously as they talked.

"How'd you like my present to you?" asked Dotty, with twinkling eyes.

"Lovely!" and Dolly smiled back. "How'd you like mine to you?"

"Beautiful! Truly, Dollyrinda, I'm awful glad to have that picture of you."

"So am I of you. Did you get any plate presents?"

"No; I didn't expect any. All the family gave me things for my room, you know. Bob sent me a dear little clock."

"How nice; Bert sent me a pair of candlesticks,—glass ones,—they're awfully pretty."

"Isn't it funny we don't know each other's brothers."

"We will soon, though. Bert is coming home in about two weeks."

"Yes, so is Bob. As soon as school closes. Oh, here come the men to put up the tent! Let's go and watch them."

Dolly had been allowed to stay at home from school for the day, and the two girls, followed by Genie, ran out on the lawn to see what was going on.

In order to make the party a truly joint affair, it had been decided to set up a tent on the lawn exactly midway between the two houses, for the party supper. It was a large tent, and gay with red trimmings and flags. Inside, tables were set up, and the maids from both houses brought out plates and glasses in abundance.

"Oh, isn't it just grand!" exclaimed Dotty, seizing Dolly round the waist and making her dance about the lawn.

"Lovely; but don't rumple me so, Dotty! This is a clean frock."

"Oh, what an old fuss you are! Always thinking about your clothes!"

"I am not, any such thing! But what's the use of spoiling a clean dress the minute you put it on?"

"All right, I'll keep away from you, if you're so afraid I'll muss you up! Proudy!"

For some unknown reason, this epithet was the most scathing in the girls' vocabulary, and either was quick to resent it.

"I am not a Proudy! And you'd look nicer if you took a little better care of your own clothes,—so there now!"

"My clothes are all right! They're as good as yours! I wish we didn't have a birthday together!"

Dotty flounced away, and Dolly walked home with an exaggerated dignity.

These little quarrels were very silly; but they often occurred between these two who were really good friends, but who sometimes acted very foolishly.

Dolly went in her own house, and as she ran upstairs, she sang so very gaily, that Mrs. Fayre looked at Trudy, and said, "Another fuss!"

"Yes," and Trudy sighed. "I don't know as Dotty Rose is a very good friend for Dolly; they quarrel a lot."

"Oh, well, they get over it right away. I think it is good for Dolly to have some one to stir her up now and then. She's naturally so meek and mild."

"Well, Dotty Rose stirs her up, all right!" and Trudy laughed.

It was about half an hour later, that Genie Rose appeared before Mrs. Fayre.

"Where's Dolly?" she demanded.

"Can't you speak a little more politely, Genie?" and Mrs. Fayre smiled pleasantly at the child.

"You ain't my mother to tell me what to say!"

"No; but this is my house and I like to have little girls act nicely here, especially as I know that you have better manners if you choose to use them."

Genie thought a moment, digging her toe into the rug, and at last said:

"Good-morning, Mrs. Fayre. Please may I see Dolly?"

"Why, what a little lady! Yes, indeed; you will find her in her room. Go right up, Genie, dear."

The child trudged upstairs, and entered Dolly's room.

"What do you want?" and Dolly, with suspiciously bright eyes, looked up from the book she was pretending to read.

"You're not so awful polite, either," and Genie's big, black eyes looked sharply at Dolly. "But never mind. I've come over to tell you that Dot's cryin' about you."

"Did she tell you to come?"

"Nope. She don't know I'm here. But I think you're two sillies to spoil your nice birthday by crying about each other."

"I'm not crying!"

26

"Well, you have been. I can see the cry-marks in your eyes. Nice blue eyes. C'mon over and make up."

"Get Dotty to come over here and make up."

"She won't come."

"Have you asked her?"

"No, but I just know she won't. So let's don't ask her, and you come over there."

"You're a funny little thing, Genie! You know a lot, don't you?"

"'Course I do. Come on, Dolly," and the child pulled at Doily's sleeve.

"All right, I will," and the two went together over to the Rose house.

Dotty in her room, heard Dolly's voice below stairs and came running down. Her anger was all past, and she was more than ready to be friends again.

"Let's go out and see the tent," said Dolly, as the two met in the hall.

"All right, let's," and out they went.

"Did you fix it up, Genie?" said her mother, who had pretty much known what was going on.

"Yes'm, I fixed it up," and Genie ran after the black puppy, who with judicial foresight was running away from her.

"Tell me about the people who are coming, Dolly," said Dotty. "Who are the nicest ones?"

"You may not like the same ones I do; but Clara Ferris is my most intimate friend of the lot."

"As intimate as I am?"

"Well, of course, I've known her so much longer, you see, she seems more intimate."

"But we're sort of twins, you know."

"Only sort of; we're not really. Well, anyway, there's Celia and then there's Maisie May."

"Maisie May! What a funny name!"

"Well, it's her name all the same. And the two Rawlins girls, Grace and Ethel."

"Are they nice?"

"Lovely. They live on the next block below us. Their brother is coming, too. Clayton, his name is."

"What other boys?"

"Oh, Reggie Stuart and Lollie Henry—"

"Lollie! What a ridiculous name for a boy!"

"His real name is Lorillard. He's an awfully nice boy. He plays the cornet in school sometimes for us to march by. Then there's Joe

Collins. He's the funniest thing! Makes you laugh all the time. And a lot of others; I can't tell you about all of them."

"Never mind; I'll catch onto them as they come. Do you think they'll like me, Dolly?"

"Of course they will; why wouldn't they?"

"I don't know; but with such a lot of them, I feel kind of shy."

"Pooh; Dot Rose, you couldn't be shy if you tried!"

"It isn't shy, exactly; but I'm afraid they won't think I'm nice."

"Oh, yes, they will; don't be silly. Anyway, some of them will. And maybe you won't like all of them. Everybody can't like everybody,—you know."

"No, I s'pose not. What do we do? Stand up to receive them?"

"Of course! Did you think we sat down? Haven't you ever had a party?"

"Not such a big one."

"Well, I've had lots of 'em. We stand side by side, and I'll introduce everybody to you. Of course, Mumsie and Trude will be around, and your mother and your aunt,—won't they? Don't try to remember all their names, 'cause you can't, and you can pick them up later."

"What a lot you know!" and Dotty looked at Dolly with a thoughtful admiration.

"I know why," said Dolly, with a sudden flash of enlightenment; "it's 'cause I have an older sister. Trudy is 'out,' you know, and I'm sort of accustomed to comp'ny; but you have a little sister, so you haven't had so much experience."

"Yes, that's it," and Dotty comprehended. "All right, you can show me, and I'll do whatever you say."

CHAPTER V

THE DOUBLE PARTY

The party was from four to seven. Before the hour the girls were in readiness and waiting on the lawn, midway between the two houses, to receive their guests.

Dolly Fayre wore a white organdie, all lacy with little ruffles and a light blue sash with blue silk stockings and white slippers.

Dotty Rose had on a lovely white voile with pink ribbons and pink stockings.

Both girls wore their hair in a long loose braid, with a big ribbon at the top of the braid.

"Didn't leave off hair-ribbons, did you?" said Dolly, smiling.

"No, Mother wouldn't hear of it. She says we ought to wear them until we're sixteen, anyway."

"I don't care much, do you?"

"No; only I'd rather leave them off. It didn't rain, you see."

"I should say not! It's a perfect day. Did you put a pink ribbon on Blot?"

"Yes, he looks lovely! Oh, here's Flossy, in her blue bow. If they'll only behave themselves!"

The puppy and the kitten had become fairly good friends, by reason of their two young mistresses' training; and frequently met without fighting, though this was not to be depended on.

"Oh, here comes somebody, Dolly! I feel as if I should run away!"

"Nonsense, Dot! don't be silly! It's only Joe Collins. Hello, Joe; this is my new friend, Dorothy Rose. It's her party, same as mine."

Joe was far from bashful. "Hay-o, Dorothy," he said, gaily. "Aren't you afraid you'll get off the line? My, but you girls are particular to stand just so!"

Dorothy flashed a smile at him. Somehow her shyness vanished, and she replied, "Oh, we only stood that way, waiting for somebody to come. Now, we can move around," and she took a few jumpy skips around the lawn. "Do you live near here?" she went on, by way of conversation.

"Couple o' blocks away. Hope we'll be friends."

"'Course we will. And I've got a brother about your size; you'll like him."

"Is he here?"

29

"No; he's away at school. Be home in about two weeks. Come and see him then."

"I will. Here come the Brown twins. Know 'em?"

"No, I don't know anybody. My! Aren't they alike?"

They certainly were, and when Dolly introduced Tod and Tad Brown, Dotty frankly stared at them.

"I never saw such twinsy twins before," she said; "do you know yourselves apart?"

"Not always," replied one of them. "But I think I'm Tod, and my brother is Tad. Of course our Sunday names are Todhunter and Tadema, but Tod and Tad are much better for every day use."

Then some girls came; Clara Ferris was among the first; and then Grace and Ethel Rawlins, and Maisie May.

Dotty took a quick liking to the last named, for she was a bright, pretty girl who seemed eager to be friends.

Clayton Rawlins came too, and Lollie Henry, and then they came in such numbers that Dotty couldn't catch all the names nor remember those she did catch.

The girls had laid off their hats and wraps in the Fayre house, and the boys in the Rose house, as every means was used to have the party equally divided.

At first they played games. The Fayres had a tennis court, and the Roses a croquet ground. Also, Mr. Rose had contributed as his "surprise" to the party a set of Lawn Bowls. This was a new sport to many of them and all liked it, and took turns at the bowling. Others wandered about the grounds or sat in the swings and hammocks, and at five o'clock they were called to supper.

Little tables had been placed on the lawn and four or six young people were seated at each. Then the good things were brought to them. Bouillon and tiny sandwiches, ices, cakes, jellies, bon-bons, everything that goes to make a delightful party supper.

The two hostesses did not sit together, and Dotty found herself with Clara Ferris, Joe Collins and one of the Brown twins.

"How do you like Berwick?" asked Tad Brown, as he finished his bouillon.

"Ever so much!" returned Dotty enthusiastically; "and now I'm acquainted with so many people I shall like it better than ever."

"Aren't you coming to school?"

"Not this term. It's so near closing, and Mother says next year I can go right into High School with Dolly Fayre."

"We'll all be in High next year," said Clara. "We're all in the same grade, you know. But I wish you would come to school now, and be in the Closing Exercises. We need more girls."

"What for?"

"Oh, for the tableaux and things. We have a splendid program. Haven't we, Tad?"

"How do you know he's Tad?" asked Dotty, laughing.

"I asked him," returned Clara. "It's the only way. Nobody can tell 'em apart."

"'Cept Mother," said Tad, grinning. "She never makes a mistake. But the teachers can't tell. I get kept in if Tod misses his lessons, and he gets marked if I'm late."

"Don't you mind?"

"No; 'cause it evens up in the long run. Tod's better-natured than I am, but I'm prettier."

"Why, how can you be?" cried Dotty; "you're exactly alike."

"Oh, I can see it! I'm much better-looking." Tad's honest, round, freckled face was winsome but not handsome, and the girls laughed at this make-believe vanity.

Dolly was at a table with the other Brown boy and Grace Rawlins and Lollie Henry.

"Dotty Rose is pretty, isn't she?" said Grace.

"Awfully pretty," agreed Dolly, "and a nice girl, too. I like her lots."

"Some looker!" declared Lollie Henry, gazing with admiration over at Dotty, who was laughing merrily.

"She's my sister," put in Genie, who was a restless spirit, and having finished her supper, was roaming around among the tables talking to different ones.

"So she is," and Dolly patted the glossy, black curls.

"Looks like a spitfire, though, if she should get mad," commented Tod Brown, who was an outspoken boy.

"Oh, I don't think so," returned Dolly; and then she remembered the few trifling quarrels they had already had. "No," she went on, "Dotty isn't a spitfire; but when she gets mad she just flounces off and gets over it."

"Just like a girl!" said Tod; "why don't you have it out, and done with it?"

"That's what Bert always says," and Dolly laughed. "I guess girls and boys are different about such things."

"I guess they are," said Grace, looking rueful. "Maisie May and I have been 'mad' for two weeks now."

"Oh, how silly!" exclaimed Lollie Henry. "I'm going to get you two girls together and make you make up!"

"Yes, let's," said Tad; "come on now; I've finished my ice cream, haven't you, Dolly?"

They all had, and they followed Tad, who was ringleader in this

31

game. The others had mostly risen from the tables, and Tad told Dolly to get Maisie and bring her over to their group.

Grace Rawlins looked a little uncertain. She honestly wanted to be friends with Maisie but she was not sure she liked the way it was being brought about.

Dolly came back, arm in arm with Maisie.

The two boys stood in front of Grace until the girls came up, and then Tad, whisking aside, said, with a low bow: "Miss Maisie May, I want to make you acquainted with Miss Grace Rawlins, the nicest girl in Berwick, except the rest of them."

Maisie coloured and looked half-angry, half-amused, and Tad went on: "I see by the papers that you two girls don't know each other to speak to, so Dolly Fayre and us two boys are a committee of three to see that you become acquainted immediately if not sooner. You two will therefore now greet each other with a nice, sweet kiss."

Tad's manner was so funny and so like a kindly old gentleman, that the girls had to laugh.

But though Grace looked willing to obey the order, Maisie did not.

"Don't be silly, Tad," she said; "I guess you don't know what Grace said about me, or you wouldn't ask me to kiss her!"

"Tell me," said Tad, with the air of an impartial judge, "and I and my wise colleague, Mr. Lorillard Henry, will size up the case and pronounce judgment."

"Why, she said I was the meanest girl in Berwick, because I wouldn't tell her the answer to an algebra example. And I couldn't, because Miss Haskell had made us all promise not to tell the answers to anybody—she wanted everybody to do them without help."

"Seems to me you did the right thing," and Tad looked at Grace.

"I didn't know that," said Grace. "I wasn't at school the day Miss Haskell said that."

"Then you couldn't be expected to know," said Tad; "now, it's just as I said, a boy would fight it out with another boy, and he might punch his head, but the matter would be understood and straightened out, and not sulk for two weeks over it."

"I didn't sulk," said Grace.

"Well, you two sillies didn't speak to each other,—it's about the same thing. Now will you be good! Will you kiss and make up?"

"I will," said Maisie May, heartily, and she flung her arms round Grace, and gave her a most friendly kiss, which was as heartily returned.

"Bless you, my children!" said Tad, dramatically. "Now don't let me hear of your quarrelling again! Are you mad at anybody, Dolly?"

"No, sir, thank you; but if I am, at any time, I'll come to you for a peacemaker."

"Oh, look who's here!" cried Lollie, spying a strange figure walking across the lawn.

The group joined the others and found themselves invited to take a seat in the rows of chairs which were lined up in front of an interesting-looking table.

They did so, and soon all present were seated in breathless anticipation of what might happen.

The tea tables had been whisked away, and at the door of the tent the stranger stood,—a table in front of him.

He was a magician, and the tricks he did held his young auditors spellbound.

Turning back his coat sleeves to prove he was concealing nothing, he would take a large sheet of white paper, and with a swift movement twirl it round into a cornucopia. This was, of course, empty, and shaking it about to prove its emptiness, he then held it upright, and invited Dolly to look into it. But he held it so high, that she had to stand on tiptoe to peep in. However, she caught a glimpse, and it seemed to her there were pink flowers in it.

Then the magician asked Dotty to peep in. She peered over the edge, and just as she exclaimed, "Why, it's full of flowers!" he overturned it on her head, and she was showered with lovely pink rosebuds made of tissue paper!

"Where did they come from?" cried everybody, as they scrambled to pick them up. "The cone was empty! Where did he get them?"

But the magician only smiled, and went on with his other tricks.

"Has any one a gold watch?" he asked.

Not many of the boys had gold watches, but Lollie Henry exhibited with pride one that his grandfather had given him on his birthday.

"May I borrow it?" said the magician; "ah, thank you," and he took it before Lollie had really consented.

"Now, a silk hat. Much obliged, sir," as Mr. Fayre provided the hat.

"Now, my young friends, we'll make an omelet. Two eggs, somebody,—please?"

Nobody had any eggs, and the magician seemed nonplussed. "What, no eggs in all this well-dressed crowd? Incredible! Ah, come here, little girl!" He caught Genie, who was running about. "Why, here is an egg in the big bow of your hair-ribbon! And here is another in the other bow! What a strange place to carry eggs! Did Mother send you to the store for them?"

"No, sir," said Genie, looking in amazement at the unmistakable eggs the man had evidently found in her ribbon. "I should think they would have dropped out sooner!"

"I should think so too," returned the magician; "lucky for me they didn't, or I could not have made the nice omelet I'm about to concoct."

He set the silk hat on the table, laid the watch and eggs beside it, and then called for a cup of milk.

Somehow or other Mrs. Fayre had that all ready and handed it to him with a smile.

"Good!" said the magician; "now we'll to work! I suppose many of you girls know how to make an omelet, so you must look sharp and see that I do it right. First, we'll break the eggs and whisk them up."

He broke the eggs right into the silk hat, and stirred them with a fork and then poured in the milk slowly, stirring all the time.

"Something else goes to an omelet," he said, trying to think; "ah, yes, some sort of an herb. Ah, I have it! Thyme! Well, well, Mr. Fayre, do you raise thyme in your kitchen garden? No? What a pity! But, luckily, I have time right here!" He took up Lollie's watch. "Ah, just, the thing!"

He threw the watch in the hat, and began to beat it with his heavy fork.

He looked anxiously in the hat. "Wants to be crushed," he said; "can't get the flavour of time unless it's crushed. Ah, here we are!" and he picked up a kitchen poker that had appeared from nowhere in particular.

With that he beat and pounded and banged the watch, and then with a big spoon, he dipped up spoonfuls of the mixture and let it run back into the hat. The children could distinctly see the bits of brass or steel wheels and springs, and even fragments of the gold case.

Lollie looked a little sober, but said no word of fear for his watch's safety.

"Now, we'll cook it," said the magician, and he poured the "omelet" into a bright, clean frying-pan.

"Where's the fire?" he asked, holding the pan high aloft, and looking all about.

"There isn't any," said Mr. Fayre; "you didn't tell me to provide a fire."

"You should have known enough for that!" shouted the magician, as if in anger. "Well, as we have no fire, of course, we can't make our omelet. So take back your things."

From the frying-pan he poured a cup of clear milk, which he

34

gave to Mrs. Fayre. Then he took out of the same pan two eggs, which he handed to Genie, intact and unbroken. Then he hesitated, saying, "What else did I borrow?"

"A watch!" "A gold watch!" cried a dozen voices.

"Oh, yes, to be sure!" and the magician, smiling, passed the pan to Lollie, and there on its clean, shining surface, lay the gold watch, absolutely unharmed.

Such a clapping of applause! for many of the young audience had been forced to believe that the watch was utterly ruined.

That closed the entertainment, and soon after that the young guests went home.

"How do you s'pose he did it?" Dolly asked of Dotty, as they sat in the swing, talking over the party.

"Oh, it's easy enough," returned Dotty. "They don't really break up the watch, you know."

"Of course I know that! But how do they do it? What becomes of the broken eggs and all?"

"I don't know, but I've seen magic tricks before and they always bring everything out right somehow!"

CHAPTER VI

ROLLER SKATING

The day after the party the two girls sat as usual in the big swing talking things over.

"I like that boy with the funny name," said Dotty; "the one they call Lollie. Such a silly name for a boy!"

"Yes; such a dignified name as Lorillard ought not to have such a silly nickname. But he's always called Lollie. He is a nice boy, but I like Joe Collins better."

"Yes, he's funny and makes you laugh all the time. But those twin boys are the nicest of all. What funny names they all have. Tod and Tad!"

"How do you like the girls?"

"The Rawlins girls are nice and Celia Ferris. But I like you best, Dolly, and except for parties I don't care so much about a crowd. Let's go roller skating."

"Oh, no; let's sit here and swing; it's too hot to skate."

"Pshaw! come on. You're too lazy for anything. You just sit around and do nothing and that's what makes you so fat. Get your skates and I'll race you around the block. Really, Doll, you ought to take more exercise or you'll get terribly fat."

"Well, you'd better not take so much then, for you're as thin as a ping-wing now!"

"What's a ping-wing?"

"I don't know, but it's the thinnest thing there is. All right, I'll skate around the block once or twice, and then we'll go and see if there are any little cakes left over from yesterday."

In a short time the two girls had their skates on and started to roll along the smooth, wide pavements of Summit Avenue.

"Let's do this," proposed Dotty. "Start right here in front of our house; you go one way and I the other round the whole block and see if we can come back and meet right straight here."

"All right, but I know I can't go as fast as you do. You skate like a streak of lightning."

"Well, I'll go sort of slow for me, and you go as swift as you can, and let's try to come together right here."

The two girls started in opposite directions, and turned their respective corners on their way around the block. In due time they passed each other in the street back of their own, and Dotty nodded approval as she saw they were about half way round. They didn't

36

pause to exchange any words but, waving their hands, went on their way and rounded again on Summit Avenue.

As they saw each other approach, they regulated their speed in a careful attempt to meet exactly where they had started. Dotty had to curb her speed and go a little more slowly or she would be ahead of time. But Dolly saw that it would take a pretty strong spurt for her to reach the goal, so when they were about ten feet apart Dolly made a special effort and put all her strength into a last grand dash. Dotty hadn't looked for this and as she rolled rather slowly to the appointed place Dolly came along and with a fell swoop, unable to control her direction, she crashed right into Dotty and the two girls went down in a heap. The impact was so sudden and unexpected that neither had a chance to save herself in any way and there was a tangle of waving arms and legs, and skate-rollers as the crash occurred.

"I've broken myself," Dolly announced calmly, though her voice sounded dazed and queer. Dotty opened her mouth to speak but changed her mind and gave voice to the wildest kind of a shriek. She followed this up with several others of increasing force and volume and looked at Dolly, wondering why she didn't yell too. But the reason was that Dolly had fainted and the white face and closed eyes of her friend made Dotty scream louder than ever.

Various members of the two families ran to the scene, as well as several neighbours.

Mrs. Fayre and Mrs. Rose looked on somewhat helplessly at the two girls, but Aunt Clara went at once at the rescue. She and Trudy lifted Dotty to her feet and found she could stand.

"Try to stop screaming, dearie," said Aunt Clara, "and tell me where you're hurt."

"I don't know," cried Dotty; "I don't know and I don't care! But Dolly is dead! My Dolly, my own Dollyrinda is dead! And it's all my fault 'cause I made her go skating, and my arm hurts awful! Ow!"

"Her arm is broken," said Mrs. Bayliss, gently lifting Dotty's right hand, which caused more piercing shrieks. "What shall we do? Somebody call a doctor quick!"

Meanwhile the strong arms of a neighbour's gardener had lifted Dolly and was carrying her toward her own home.

"It's her leg that's bruk," he said, holding her as gently as possible. "It's good luck she fainted; she'll come round all right, but she's bruk a bone, the poor dear."

It seemed ages to the anxious mothers and friends, but it was really only a short time before doctors arrived and the two little sufferers were put to bed and their injuries attended to.

Sure enough Dolly's leg was broken, and Dotty had a fractured arm.

Both houses were in a tumult of confusion as surgeons and nurses took possession and bones were set and splints and bandages applied.

Dolly Fayre took it quietly and seemed almost awestricken, when at last she realised that she was in her bed to stay for several weeks.

"But it doesn't hurt much," she said wonderingly to Trudy. "Why does it take so long to get well?"

"Because the bone has to knit, dear, and that is a slow process. I'm glad it doesn't hurt, but it may at times. The worst, though, is that you will get very tired lying still so long. But I know what a brave little girl you are, and we will all do all we can to help and amuse you."

"Did Dotty break anything?"

"Yes, she broke her left arm. That is not as bad as your breaking your leg, for she can walk about sooner than you can. But hers is more painful, so there's small choice in the two accidents."

"Is she yelling like fury?" inquired Dolly, who herself lay placid and white-faced, though her blue eyes showed the strain she had undergone.

"Yes, she is," and Trudy smiled a little. "You two children are so different. I wish you would yell a little and not look so patiently miserable."

"What's Dolly yelling about? Because she hurts so?"

"Partly that; and partly because she's blaming herself for the whole thing."

"How ridiculous! She isn't a bit more to blame than I am. She proposed skating, but it was because I ran into her that we fell down. I tried to steer out but I couldn't."

"Don't think about who is to blame; that doesn't matter. The only thing to think about is to get well as quick as you can."

"But we can't do anything to help that along; the doctors have to do that."

"Indeed you can help a lot. If you're patient and quiet and cheerful you will get well sooner than if you fuss and fret and cry. That might cause fever and inflammation and all sorts of things."

Trudy was sitting on the edge of Dolly's bed and she smiled lovingly down at her little sister. "I'm going to take care of you," she went on; "Mother wants to have a trained nurse, but I think you would like it better to have me for a nurse, wouldn't you?"

"I'd like it better," and Dolly looked up wistfully, "but I don't want to bother you too much, Trudy."

"Oh, it isn't any bother, and besides, Mother will do a great deal of the nursing. Here she comes now with your luncheon."

Mrs. Fayre came in, bringing a dainty tray on which was a small bowl of broth and some crackers.

"The nurse has gone," she announced, "and I'm glad of it. It was necessary to have her here while the doctors set the broken bones, and she will come in every morning as long as may be necessary. But it's much nicer to be in charge of this case myself and have full jurisdiction over my patient."

"Oh, ever so much nicer, Mother," and Dolly raised affectionate blue eyes to her mother's face. "Can I sit up to eat?"

"No, honey; you'll have to learn to eat lying down. But Mother will feed you and we'll pretend you're one of those grand Roman ladies who always ate their meals reclining on a couch."

So, although not altogether a comfortable procedure, Dolly took her first lesson in swallowing without raising her head.

Meantime somewhat different scenes were being enacted next door.

Dotty's more excitable nature had been thoroughly upset by the shock of the accident, the pain of her injury and the remorse that she felt at feeling herself responsible for the tragedy.

Her screams were hysterical and the efforts of her mother, her aunt and the nurse to quiet her were alike unavailing.

"I've killed my Dolly! I've killed my Dolly!" she would cry over and over, and though they told her that Dolly Fayre was resting quietly and suffering very little pain, she would not believe it and insisted they were deceiving her.

"You only say that to quiet me!" she cried. "I know it isn't true. I know Dolly has broken most all her bones and I know she'll never walk again. Why, I saw her myself, all limp and dead-looking. If she lives she'll be a cripple. Oh, my arm! my arm! I wish they'd cut it off! I'd rather not have it at all than have it hurt like this."

Impulsive Dotty tried to move her injured arm and then shrieked with the pain it caused her.

"You mustn't do that!" said Nurse Johnson somewhat severely; "if you try to move that arm it won't heal right and you'll have to have it broken over again and re-set."

Dotty glared at the nurse and then screamed: "I hate you! You go right straight out of this house! My mother can take care of me good enough and I don't want you around."

"There, there, Dotty dear," said Mrs. Rose; "don't talk to nurse like that. She has been very kind to you; and it's true if you move your arm around like that or try to do so, you'll make your injury far worse."

39

"I don't care! I want to make it worse! I want to have it cut off! I won't have a broken arm,— I won't— I won't!"

"Don't mind her, nurse; she's beside herself with pain and fright."

"Oh, that's all right, Mrs. Rose," and the white-capped nurse smiled; "I don't blame little girls for being cantankerous when they're laid up like this. It's awful hard on them and nobody knows it better than I do. And I'm not going to stay long, Miss Dotty. Only a day or two till your mother and aunt get the knack of taking care of you."

"I shall be head nurse," said Mrs. Bayliss, smiling at Dotty, "and your mother shall be my assistant."

"I don't want you for my nurse, Aunt Clara, and I don't want Miss Johnson, I just want Mother all the time."

"Yes, Dotty, dear, Mother will be here all the time," and Mrs. Rose gently stroked the moist dark curls back from the little brow.

For a few moments Dotty was quieter, and then she screamed out again, "Tell me about Dolly, tell me the truth about Dolly. Did she break both her legs?"

"No, dear, only one. It has been set and she is doing nicely, although she will be in bed for a long time. You will probably get up and go to see her long before she can come in here."

"I want to go now!" and Dotty tried to rise; "I want to see Dolly! I must see Dolly!"

Gently but firmly the nurse held Dotty down on the pillows. "Lie still," she commanded, for she saw that stern measures were necessary.

"I can't lie still, when I don't know how Dolly is! I don't believe what you tell me about her. But I'll believe Genie. She always tells me the truth. Come here, Genie!"

Dotty screamed her sister's name in a loud voice, and the little girl came running into the sick room.

Genie looked scared and white-faced as she saw Dotty in splints and bandages.

"Genie," said Dotty, and her black eyes burned like coals, "you go straight over to Fayres and see Dolly. See for yourself and see just how she is and come straight back and tell me."

"Let her go," said the nurse; "that's a good idea."

So Genie ran over to the next house and found Mrs. Fayre.

"Please let me see Dolly," she said earnestly, "'cause if I don't Dotty thinks she's dead, and then Dotty will die too, so please let me see her, Mrs. Fayre. Can't I?"

After some consideration Mrs. Fayre said Genie might go to Dolly's room for a few moments.

"How are you, Dolly?" said the child, marching in and standing by the bedside with the air of a Royal Messenger.

"I'm pretty good," and Dolly smiled wanly at her little visitor. "How's Dotty?"

"Dotty's awful. But she'll be better when she knows how you are. So tell me zactly."

"Well, tell Dotty my right leg is broken. One of the bones just above the ankle. But tell her except for that, I'm all right and for her not to worry about me and we'll see who can get well first. And give her my love and—and—oh, that's all, good-bye, Genie!"

The little girl ran out of the room and as soon as she disappeared Dolly burst into floods of weeping. That was her way of relieving her overburdened nerves instead of screaming hysterically like Dotty.

Trudy tried to soothe her, but there was no staying the torrent of tears, until at last they stopped because Dolly was exhausted.

"There," said Mrs. Fayre brightly as she wiped Dolly's eyes, "I'm just glad you did that! There's nothing like a good cry to straighten things out. Now I shouldn't be one bit surprised if you could take a nice little nap." And Dolly did so.

Meantime Genie trotted home with her comforting news for Dotty.

"Dolly's all right," she announced. "'Cept one leg is broked. But that's all. Only just one bone of one leg. And she says to see who'll get well first."

"How did she look?" asked Dotty eagerly.

"Like a angel," replied Genie, enthusiastically. "Her face was all white and her eyes were so blue and her hair was all goldy and braided in two curly braids tickling around her ears. Oh, she looked lovely! Heaps better than you do, Dot. Your face is all red and splotchy, and your eyes are as big as saucers and your hair looks like the dickens."

"I don't care," said Dotty, crossly; "I don't care how I look."

"But I care how you feel," said her mother, "and now you know that Dolly is very much alive, I'm sure you'll let nurse bathe your face and brush your hair and then I'm going to sing you to sleep."

As is usual in case of broken bones the first night proved a very trying time for all concerned.

Dolly Fayre, though an unusually patient child, felt as if she could not bear the pain and discomfort of her strapped and splinted leg. Her mother and Trudy, and her father too, did all they could to alleviate her sufferings, but the uncontrollable tears welled up in the blue eyes and rolled over the fevered cheeks of the little sufferer.

41

"I try to be good, Father," she said, as Mr. Fayre bent over her, "but it does hurt so awful."

"Does it, you dear blessed baby? Let Daddy cuddle your head in his arm, so, and sing to you, maybe that will help."

But when Mr. Fayre gently put his arm under the golden head on the pillow Dolly cried out that his coat sleeve was too scratchy.

"Well, now, we'll just fix that! Give me one of your dressing gowns, Mother."

Dolly had to laugh a little when Mrs. Fayre brought a silk kimono of her own and managed to get its loose folds draped around her stalwart husband.

"Now I rather guess we won't scratch our poor little fevery cheeks," and Mr. Fayre so deftly slipped his silk clad arm under Dolly's head, that she rested in his strong clasp with a feeling of security and comfort.

"That's lovely, Daddy; it just seems as if I had some of your big strong strength and my pain doesn't hurt so much."

Then Mr. Fayre sang in soft low tones which greatly soothed the little patient. But not for long. All through the night the paroxysms of agony would recur and poor little Dolly cried like a baby, because she couldn't possibly help it.

But the Rose family had even worse times to take care of Dotty. She, too, suffered intensely and even made it worse because she wouldn't stay still. With a sudden jerk she would sit up in bed and then scream with the pain occasioned by wrenching her injured arm.

"You mustn't do that, dear," said Mr. Rose, who usually could calm Dotty in her most wilful moments.

"I have to!" cried the little girl; "you would, too, if your arm was all on fire, and shooting needles into you and not set right and has to be broken over again and all twisted up and hanging by a thread, anyway! Ow!—ow!—OW!!" Her voice rose in a shrill screech and she rocked back and forth in her pain and anger.

"Now, Dotty dear," said her father, "you must realise that you make matters a great deal worse by jumping around and moving your arm—"

"But I can't help it! I'm going to shake it till I shake it off!" and Dotty gave a violent shake of her shoulders and then screamed with the added pain she brought on herself.

She so disarranged the bandages that it was necessary to telephone for the doctor at once to readjust them.

"This won't do, young lady," said Dr. Milton as he looked at the havoc she had wrought in his careful work; "if you keep up these performances you'll have to be strapped to the bed so tightly that you can't move either arm. How would you like that?"

"I'd break loose somehow! you shan't strap me down!" Dotty's eyes blazed and her black curls bobbed as she shook her head angrily at the doctor.

But Dr. Milton paid little heed to her words. He redressed her arm and then said in his firm yet pleasant way: "I don't know you very well, Miss Dotty, but I perceive you have a strong will of your own. Now are you going to use it rightly to help yourself get well, or wrongly to make all the trouble possible for yourself and every one else?"

Dotty looked at him. She was not accustomed to this kind of talk, for her parents were inclined to be over indulgent with her tantrums and her temper.

"I do want to get well as soon as I can," she said, "and I will try to be good,—but you don't know how it hurts."

"Yes, I do know," and the good doctor smiled down at her; "I know it hurts like fury! like the very dickens and all! and I know it's just all you can do to bear it. But if you can get through to-night, I'll promise you it'll feel better to-morrow."

He went away and Dotty did try to be as good as she could, but the awful twinges of pain frequently made her forget her resolutions and to herself and the whole household it seemed as if the night would never end.

CHAPTER VII

TWO BIG BROTHERS

"Whoop-oo! Whoop-ee! Hoo-ray!! Where are you? Hey! Hi!!"

With half a dozen steps, Bob Rose ran up the staircase of his new home in Berwick, to Dotty's room.

As he had been at school when the family moved he had never seen the house before, and now, the school term over, he had come home for vacation and his first thought was for his broken-armed sister.

It was two weeks since the accident, but Dotty was still in bed. Her arm was doing nicely, but she was such a nervous and excitable child that it was thought best to keep her as quiet as possible. She was sitting up in a nest of pillows and a rose coloured kimono was draped round her bound-up arm. But she waved the other hand gaily as Bob dashed into the room.

"Well, old girl," he cried, "this is the limit! The idea of your smashing yourself like this! Here I've played every old kind of ball and everything else and never broke one of my two hundred and eight blessed bones! And you just go out on lady-like roller skates and come a cropper. Fie upon you! does it hurt much?"

"You bet it hurts, Bob! Nothing like it did at first, but it hurts a good deal, and it's awful uncomfortable. I can't move it, you know, and I can't do hardly anything for myself."

"Pooh! pshaw! of course you can do things for yourself. What a chump you are, Dot. Why it's your left arm, you ought to be able to do everything in creation with your right arm alone, except maybe play the piano or clap your hands. I'll show you how to do things. Is your right arm all right?"

"Yes, I s'pose so, but I haven't used it any."

"Jiminy crickets, isn't that just like a girl! Honest, Dot, I thought you'd have more spunk. But I'll put you through, with bells on!"

Bob Rose, just turned eighteen, was a boyish duplicate of Dotty. He had the same snapping black eyes and his hair though short had a curly twist to it which, though he hated it himself made a becoming frame for his handsome face. He was overflowing with mischief and life and was devoted to athletic or outdoor sports of all kinds. He was very fond of his sister and the two had always been great chums, though frequently indulging in spirited quarrels.

"What's this place like, anyway?" he inquired, as he sat on the edge of Dotty's bed and draped his long arm over the footboard. "You've got a jolly room all right," and he looked round admiringly at the pretty rose and grey effects.

"Yes, isn't it lovely! It was my birthday present,—the furnishings, I mean. I wrote you about it, you know. We were going to fix up a lovely room for you, too, but after I broke my arm, Mother and Aunt Clara didn't have time to do anything but tend to me."

"Well, they'll catch time now. I want a room fixed up for me as good as yours,—but not so dinky-fussy. I'll pick out the things myself. You needn't think you own the whole shooting-match, Miss Dotty-Doodles! I just guess Brother Bob home on his vacation will come in for his share of attention! You won't be neglected, I'll look out for that, but just remember that I'm here, too. What's the town like?"

"I don't know myself much. You see we had our party and I met a lot of the boys and girls and then the very next day I smashed myself and of course I haven't seen any of them since."

"But you can pretty soon now. Why, it's only your arm, your legs are all right, you can walk, can't you? Why don't you go downstairs and have people come to see you?"

"I couldn't see people in a dressing-gown!"

"Well, Mother can rig you up a basque or a polonaise or something. Or put on a raincoat or an Indian blanket,—but for goodness' sake get out and around. I'll stir you up—"

"Here, here, what's going on?" and Mrs. Rose came in just in time to hear Bob's last words. "You're not to stir Dotty up, Bob, we want to keep her quiet."

"Quiet nothing! She'll dry up and blow away if she doesn't get a move on! You're going to rig her up some sort of civilian dress Mother and get her downstairs this very day. She's not sick or going into a decline, is she?"

The influence of Bob's breezy chatter had wrought a change in Dotty. During the two weeks that had just passed she had become peevish and fretful from enforced inactivity and now the thought of getting up and going downstairs had brought the smiles to her face and the light to her eyes.

Moreover, Mrs. Rose was impressed also by the determination of her big young son and began to think that perhaps his way might be right after all.

"Now you've got to tend to me, Mumsie," Bob said in his wheedlesome way, as he caressed his mother in a big bearish fashion. "You've got to fix up a room for me, all just as I want it, and you've got to make me chocolate cakes and all sorts of good things to eat, and you've got to do lots of things for your prodigal son. Dotty has had her turn and now it's mine, but while you're busy about me, I'll look after Dot, bless her old heart!" And Bob blew a kiss from his finger tips to his pretty sister who had already begun to take a new interest in life.

"Hello, Aunt Clara," Bob called out as Mrs. Bayliss passed through the hall, "come in here and help us dressmakers. Can't you rig up a costume for Dot that will be presentable to wear downstairs?"

"Downstairs!" exclaimed Aunt Clara; "did the doctor say she could go down?"

"Dr. Bob said so!" and the boy laughed. "I know all about broken arms, and there's no use giving in to them too much. The more you do for them, the more you may. Now Dotty is going to forget hers and have just as good a time as if she never broke it. I say, Dot, how's that chum of yours, you wrote me about? Is this her picture? Wow! Ain't she the peach!"

Bob picked up the picture of Dolly from Dotty's dressing-table and admired it openly. "Does she really look like that?"

"Yes," and Dotty waxed enthusiastic; "she's beautiful. Just like a pinky rose with blue eyes."

"She broke her leg didn't she, in your all-comers' scrap?"

"Yes; she can't move for six weeks."

"Well, two weeks are gone now, that's something. Can't I see her? I'd like to sympathise."

"Oh, yes, Bob, of course you must see her, but I don't want you to go over there till I can go with you."

"Oh, I'm not going to wait for that. I must have a peep at this blue-eyed fairy for myself. Any go to her?"

"Not much," and Dotty smiled. "Dolly's a perfect dear, but she's slow."

"All right, we'll have to hurry her along a little. When does her brother come home? Have you ever seen him? What's he like?"

"He's coming day after to-morrow. No, I've never seen him, but Dolly thinks he just about made the world."

"Well, I'll reserve my opinion till I see the bunch. Honest, old girl, I'm glad you're getting along as well as you are, but I'm going to do wonders for you. It's going to be lucky for you that you've got Brother on the job. Why, Dot, we were all going camping this summer, you know, what about that?"

"We haven't planned for the summer yet, Bobs," said his mother. "Perhaps by August, if Dotty is all right, we can go somewhere for awhile."

"You bet we will!" returned Bob. "Dotty will be all right!"

46

The next day but one Mrs. Rose took her big boy over to call on Dolly Fayre.

Though unable to leave her bed, Dolly could sit up and was allowed to see a few visitors each day. It was her nature to be quiet, so she was a much more tractable patient than Dotty and her broken bone had already begun to knit and was getting along nicely. It was very monotonous to sit or lie there day after day, but Dolly was patient and always took things placidly. Her parents and Trudy read to her and played games with her and entertained her in various ways and Dolly was as cheerful as any little girl could be in such circumstances.

It was a bitter disappointment to her that she could not take part in the Closing Exercises of her class. But she was reconciled to her fate and made no complaints, though deeply regretting her enforced absence from school. Her classmates came to see her occasionally, but they were so busy preparing for the celebration that they had little time for social calls.

Dotty looked forward eagerly to the homecoming of her brother Bert and she also awaited with some curiosity the meeting with Bob Rose.

However, she had heard so much about Bob from Dotty, that she was not surprised when the merry-faced boy appeared at her bedside with a gay and cheery greeting.

"I'm Bob," he said, holding out his hand, and not waiting for his mother's more formal introduction.

"I'm Dolly," and the blue eyes smiled at him as a little white hand clasped his own.

"By Jove, you do look like your picture, only you're prettier!" exclaimed Bob as he took the chair Mrs. Fayre offered him.

"It's my new cap," and Dolly smiled from beneath the lacy frills and rosebud decorations of a dainty new cap that Trudy had just made for her. She wore a Japanese kimono of pale green silk embroidered with white cherry blossoms, and as she sat surrounded by embroidered pillows and lace coverlets, Bob thought he had never seen a prettier picture.

"You look like a princess," he said. "Princess Dolly."

"I am a princess," she smiled back; "Mother and Trudy are my ladies in waiting and do just as I bid them. How much you look like Dotty."

"Glad you think so; I think Dot's a raving beauty. But I say, it's a shame you two girls had to go and break each other up just when we were going to have a perfectly good old summer time."

"I know it; isn't it a shame. But we'll have to wait till next summer and have the fun then."

47

"'Deed we won't! You'll be outdoors by the first of August, won't you?"

"Yes," and Dolly made a wry face, "but that's about the same as saying the first of Eternity!"

"Oh, not so bad as that. And anyhow I'm an inventive genius, and I'll bet we can have some fun even before August."

A bustle and commotion was heard downstairs just then and Dolly's face lighted up as she heard a familiar voice.

"Oh," she cried; "there's Bert! Come on up, Bert."

"Sure thing!" came the reply, and in another minute Bert Fayre stood in the doorway.

He was a tall, slender boy of seventeen with brown hair and eyes and he looked at Dolly with a pained expression.

"Poor old Doll!" he said softly; "I'm so sorry for you!"

"Oh, it isn't very bad now, Bert," and Dolly smiled cheerfully. "Come on in and meet Mrs. Rose and Bob. They're our next door neighbours."

Bert came in and greeted the visitors with an easy grace. Then going over to Dolly he kissed her affectionately and sat down beside her.

The two boys silently sized each other up and each concluded that the other seemed to be "A little bit of all right."

They attended different schools, and soon were deep in a discussion of their school doings. Dolly lay back among her pillows and looked at them. She adored her brother and she decided that Dotty's brother was also worthy of consideration. She liked Bob's breezy offhand way which was not at all like Bert's gentle, kindly manner. But they were two awfully nice boys and she felt sure they were going to be friends. If only she could be up and around and have good times with them! A slight pang of envy swept over her, as she heard Bob enthusiastically declare that he was going to have Dot out of bed and downstairs in short order. For no amount of enthusiasm or energy could work that miracle for Dolly, in less than a month. But she did not show this disappointment and chatted gaily with the boys and with Mrs. Rose and her own mother.

As the days went by the four young people became good friends. The boys were chummy from the first and nearly every day they carried messages back and forth for the girls. But there were long hours when the girls were alone, and both patient Dolly and impatient Dotty deeply wished they had never tried that roller-skate race.

"There's no use celebrating the Fourth of July," said Bert disconsolately, a few days before the Fourth. "We don't want a celebration that the girls can't see."

"Then let's have one that they can see," said Bob; "I'll tell you what we'll do,—I've a brilliant idea."

His idea was a brilliant one, so much so that it required the co-operation of both families with the exception of the two girls, from whom it was kept a secret.

But the two D's were told that the evening of the Fourth would be a red letter day for them and they looked forward eagerly to whatever it might be.

About seven o'clock on Fourth of July evening, Mrs. Fayre came into Dolly's room with her arms full of red, white and blue material. This proved to be a voluminous robe-like drapery which transformed Dolly into a goddess of liberty. A liberty cap was put upon her golden head and a silk flag was presented to her.

"Stunning!" exclaimed Bert, who came in to view the effect. "Just you wait, old girl, and we'll bring you something you'll like better yet!"

So Dolly waited and in a few moments she could hear out in the hall much giggling and many footsteps. Then Trudy came in and arranged a screen so that the doorway from the hall was hidden. Dolly watched breathlessly and soon heard people coming in behind the screen and recognised the boys' voices as well as those of her father and Mr. Rose.

"I know you're there, Bob and Bert," she called out. "Come here Bob and see the goddess of liberty."

"Wait a minute," said Bert, and there was more giggling and whispering.

"Now!" said somebody and then the screen was whisked away and Dolly saw standing before her,—Dotty!

It really was Dotty, smiling with eagerness and dressed like Dolly in red, white and blue.

"Oh, Dotty!" and "Oh, Dolly!" rang out at the same moment and the two girls stared hard at each other, for they had not seen one another's faces since that fatal moment when they came together on their roller skates.

"I'm just crazy to run over there and grab you!" cried Dotty, "but I promised I wouldn't touch you, or I might break us up all over again."

"Well, do come over here and sit beside me, so I can be sure it's really you. How is your arm? Does it hurt you now? Oh, what a beautiful sling!"

Dotty's left arm was in a large sling made of dark blue studded with silver stars and her whole dress was of red and white stripe. Her liberty cap was just like Dolly's own, and she wore white stockings and red slippers.

"You poor dear," she said as she came over and sat down by Dolly's side; "to think I can dress and go outdoors while you're still tied to your bed."

"But I can wave both arms about, and you can't," said Dolly as she waved her flag above her head.

"I think you're six of one and half a dozen of the other," said Bert. "Now look here, Doll, we're going to push your bed up to the window so you can see out."

"Why?" asked Dolly; "it's almost dark now."

"Never you mind. Little girls shouldn't ask questions. Grab that other bed-post, Bob. Here, Dad, take hold of the head-board."

Propelled by willing arms the bed was rolled over to the big bay window and arranged so that Dolly had full view of the lawn between the houses.

Then a big easy chair was arranged for Dotty and the two girls were advised that if they would stay there they would see something worth while.

"Oh, it's so good to see you again," said Dotty, as the others all left the room; "do you hurt terribly?"

"Not so much now, but it was awful at first. Wasn't yours?"

"Oh, terrible. Let's not talk about it. How do you like Bob?"

"He's splendid. How do you like Bert?"

"I think he's great. Oh, Dolly, what fun we could have if we were only well."

"You are. You can go outdoors."

"Not much. This is a special dispensation to-night. And I have to have my arm in a sling four weeks longer. It's in splints you know. I can't do hardly anything with one hand. Bob tries to teach me, but I'm as awkward as a cow. I'm so used to flying at everything with both hands that I can't seem to manage."

"It must be awful. Oh, Dot, there's a sky rocket!"

Dotty turned quickly and looked out of the window. The skyrocket was only the beginning of a fine display of fireworks. Mr. Rose and Mr. Fayre had concluded that was the only sort of celebration the girls could enjoy, so they had bought far more than their usual supply and they made a fine showing.

Bob had asked a number of the young people to come and see them and Dolly and Dotty recognised many from their post of observation in the window.

But the mothers of the two girls would not let any of the young people go up to Dotty's room lest the excitement be too much for her.

After the usual quota of rockets and Roman candles there were

50

more elaborate pieces which flamed into fire pictures against the summer sky.

When the fireworks were all over and the young people gone away the girls were told that there was a little more celebration yet to come.

Dolly's bed was pushed back to its place and Dotty was enthroned beside it in her easy chair, when the two boys appeared, each bearing a tray of good things.

"This is your Fourth of July party," said Trudy, who followed. "No one can come to it except the three Roses and the three Fayres."

Genie came in then, and the six brothers and sisters of the two families had a merry feast while their elders remained downstairs.

"It's been a beautiful holiday," said Dolly, leaning back into her pillows as she finished her ice cream. "I never dreamed I'd have any Fourth of July celebration. The fireworks were beautiful and the party things were lovely, but best of all is seeing Dotty again."

"Yes," said Dotty, "I don't know how I've managed to live through the last three weeks. But I expect I can come over to see you every day now."

"We'll see about that," said Mrs. Rose, coming in. "But this party must break up now, and if it doesn't do any harm to our wounded soldiers we may allow more of them. So say good-night, you two D's, and I'll take my little goddess of liberty home."

51

CHAPTER VIII

CROSSTREES CAMP

The summer plans of the two families were decidedly changed by the accidents to the two little girls.

It was the custom of the Fayres to spend the summer at a hotel in the mountains or at the seashore, for Mrs. Fayre declared she needed a yearly rest from housekeeping duties.

The Rose family, preferring a different sort of enjoyment, spent their summers at their camp in the Adirondacks, for they loved the informal out of door life and the freedom from all conventionalities.

The doctor had said that the two girls would be entirely restored to health and strength and quite ready to go anywhere by the first of August, but not much before that date. So during July the question was discussed frequently and at length as to where Dotty and Dolly would go, for they begged and besought their parents that they might be together.

Now Mrs. Rose was more than willing to take Dolly to camp with her family, and Mrs. Fayre would have been very glad to have Dotty with them at the hotel, but neither mother wanted her own little girl to go away from her. The question seemed very difficult of decision, for the two families could not agree upon a summer resort that would please them both.

But after many long talks and various suggested plans it was finally decided that Dolly Fayre should go with the Roses for the first two weeks of August and that Dotty Rose should spend the last two weeks of the month with the Fayre family.

"It is the best plan," said Mrs. Rose, "for a fortnight in camp will do the girls lots of good and make them strong and rosy again. Then they will better enjoy a fortnight at a big hotel."

The two D's were enchanted at the prospect.

"You'll just love it!" said Dotty, enthusiastically; "we'll just wear short skirts and middy blouses, and spend all our time in the woods or on the lake."

Dolly wanted to go to the camp, but she had never before been away from her mother for more than a day or two at a time, and she felt some misgivings about being homesick.

"Nonsense!" said Bert. "A great big girl like you homesick! Why, Towhead, you're too big for such things. You'll have a gorgeous time in the camp, there's more fun in a camp than in any other place on earth. I wish they had asked me."

"Of course they wouldn't ask you," said Dolly, "because Bob Rose won't be there. Not at first, anyway; he's going to visit some school friend. He's going to the camp later. But Bob, what's a camp like? Don't you have to sleep on old dry twigs and things? I want to be with Dotty, but I don't believe I'll like sleeping in a tent or whatever they have."

"Ah, be a sport, Towhead. You're altogether too finicky about your foolish comforts. Learn to rough it,—it'll be good for you. You're as white as a sheet, and you ought to be all brown and red and freckled and look like a real live girl instead of a wax doll. I'm going to coax Dad to go camping next year. It's loads of fun. Maybe if Bob Rose gets up there before you leave they'd ask me up for a couple of days."

"Or they might ask you after I've left," said Dolly; "you boys could have a lot of fun even if we girls weren't there."

"You bet we could! Girls are not a necessity to a fellow's pleasure if he has fishing and boating and swimming and such things to do."

"Well, I can't swim and I hate to fish,—but I do like boating. What kind of boats will they have, Bob?"

"Oh, motor boats and canoes and rowboats and sail boats and every old kind. Don't get drowned, Dolly, and don't break any more of your bones, but I guess there's nothing much else that can happen to you, if you behave yourself. But don't try to do everything Dotty suggests. She's a hummer, that girl, and I'll bet you in camp she'll run wild. You'll have to hold her back a little."

Dolly's parents gave her practically the same advice. But they felt little fear of Dolly's likelihood of rushing into madcap adventures even if Dotty urged it. For Dolly was slow of movement and slower still in making up her mind; while Dotty was quick as a flash in thought and action.

Mrs. Fayre sighed a little as she selected Dolly's wardrobe. She dearly loved to array her pretty daughter in muslins and organdies with dainty laces and ribbons; but camp life called for stout frocks of tweed or gingham, heavy walking boots and no fripperies.

"I shall put in one or two pretty dresses," Mrs. Fayre said, "in case you are invited to a party or any such affair. And the rest of your summer things I will have ready for you, when you come back and join us at the seashore."

And so the first of August, Mr. and Mrs. Rose and their two daughters with Dolly as the guest started for the Crosstrees Camp.

It was a sad parting between Dolly and her mother and at the last Dolly declared flatly she would not go, and throwing herself in her mother's arms burst into tears.

53

"Rubbish!" cried Rob, who was dancing about in his efforts to get Dolly started. "I'm ashamed of you, Towhead! Brace up now, and have a nerve. One final wrench and off you go!"

The boy literally tore Dolly from Mrs. Fayre's arms and boosted her in to the Roses' motor car which was waiting to take them to the station.

"All aboard! Go ahead!" Bob called out, waving his hand to the chauffeur and the car started off at a brisk rate.

"You know you needn't go, Dolly, even yet, if you don't want to," and Mrs. Rose smiled kindly at the little girl, as they flew down the avenue.

"I do want to go, Mrs. Rose, and I am ashamed of myself for acting so bad, but I will brace up now. It was just saying good-bye to Mother that somehow sort of seemed to shake my heart."

Dolly smiled through her tears and determinedly began to chatter gaily.

"That's the ticket!" said Mr. Rose, smiling approval at her. "That's the brave little girl. Now when you get to Crosstrees you'll be so delighted and interested, that you won't think of home and Mother for two weeks, except to write a postcard now and then."

"You won't hardly have time for that!" cried Dotty, "there's so much to do from morning till night, and that makes you so tired that you sleep from night till morning. Oh, Dollyrinda, we will have the most gorgeousest times ever!"

"It's beautiful to have Dolly with us," said Genie, her big black eyes dancing with anticipation; "we can show her all our fav'rite places, and all the islands and woodses and everything! But two weeks is an awful short time."

"We'll make it longer next year," said Mr. Rose. "If our two wounded soldiers hadn't been wounded, we would have started a month ago."

"Why do you call it Crosstrees camp?" asked Dolly.

"You'll see when you get there," and Mr. Rose smiled at his little visitor.

Sure enough when they arrived, Dolly discovered the meaning of the strange name. The gateway was formed by two trees which had started to grow parallel, but in some way had been bent toward one another until their trunks crossed about ten feet above ground. The trees had gone on growing this way, and formed an "N," covered with branches and foliage. The party had landed from their train at a small station near one end of a long lake. They had traversed this lake in a swift motor boat, for their camp was at the other end. It was nearly dark when they reached their own pier and all clambered out and climbed a flight of narrow wet steps.

"Hang on to the railing, Doll," said Dotty; "the steps are slippery, a little."

Passing under the crosstrees, to which Mr. Rose drew Dolly's attention as the name of the camp, they came to a sort of bungalow or long, low house.

"Is this the camp?" said Dolly, in surprise. "I thought it was tents. You said so, Dot."

"There are tents, too. Only on stormy nights we sleep inside. Come on in, Doll. Isn't it fine?"

Dolly Fayre looked around at the bare boarded rooms, the scant furniture and rough walls of the cabin, for it was little more than that.

She was cold and rather hungry, but underneath these discomforts was a far more troublesome one which she tried not to think about, but which she felt sure was going to develop into an acute case of homesickness.

"Run up to your rooms, girlies, and take off your things," said Mrs. Rose, cheerily. "We'll eat inside to-night, and Maria will make us some of her good flap-jacks for supper."

Maria was an old coloured servant and the only one who accompanied the Rose family to camp. Other help that might be needed they procured from some of the natives who were glad to do odd jobs for the summer people.

Dolly followed Dotty and Genie upstairs where there was a long row of tiny bedrooms opening onto a narrow hall. These bedrooms had ceilings which slanted right down to the floor, so one could not stand upright after advancing a few feet into the room.

"Aren't they funny rooms?" said Dotty, laughing with glee at Dolly's blank-looking countenance. "But you'll get used to them soon. Of course you have to bend double, except just here by the door, but that's nothing. This one is yours, Dolly, and mine is right next and then Genie's. Mother and Father have a room downstairs. But we won't sleep here, we'll sleep in the open tent to-night, it's plenty warm enough. Oh, it's such fun!"

Dolly didn't know what sleeping in an open tent meant, but she smiled in response and soon the three girls went downstairs together.

Mr. and Mrs. Rose were bustling around, happily engaged in unpacking and arranging books and pictures and various trifles to make the big living-room more homelike.

"Looks a little bare now," said Mr. Rose, as he placed his smoking set in position near his own particular easy chair, "but in a day or two we'll have it looking like a little Paradise on earth. Just

55

you wait, Miss Dolly, till you see this desert blossom like a rose,—like a whole Rose family, in fact!"

"These things help a lot," and Mrs. Rose deftly arranged half a dozen sofa pillows on a big inviting-looking couch.

"And to-morrow we'll put up a swing, and the hammocks, won't you, Daddy?" said Genie.

"Course I will, chickabiddy," and Mr. Rose whistled in gay contentment as he took books from their boxes and arranged them on the table.

When supper was announced, Maria informed the family that she hadn't been able to manage the flap-jacks that night.

"But you-all sho'ly will hab 'em for breakfast, dat you will,—you suttinly will. But you see huccum I jes' didn't hab de proper contraptions unpacked for 'em to-night."

"That's all right, Maria," said Mr. Rose, good-naturedly; "we don't mind what we have to-night. To-morrow we'll get a good fair start. Sit down, children, we'll manage to make out a supper."

The supper was sort of a makeshift of sardines and herring and crackers, with coffee for the older people.

Dolly had no wish to be critical, but the viands were not tempting and she ate very little, being conscious all the time of an ever-growing lump in her throat. She tried hard to be merry and gay, but she couldn't feel the enthusiasm with which the others overflowed.

"Shall we have a fire to-night, Daddy?" asked Dotty as they left the table.

"Oh, not to-night. It's pretty late, and we're all tired out. We'll leave that for to-morrow night. You see, Dolly Fayre, the curtain doesn't really rise on the glories of Camp Crosstrees until to-morrow. Can you wait?"

"Yes, indeed, Mr. Rose," and Dolly smiled bravely. "Where is it that we're going to sleep?"

"I'll show you," said Mrs. Rose, and amid shouts of glee and peals of laughter, Dotty and Genie ran upstairs, and returned with their arms full of blankets and other things.

"Grab a pillow and come on," shouted Dotty as she herself picked up a pillow from the couch. Genie took one, too, and Dolly did also and then the whole tribe left the house.

They walked across some very uneven ground and Dolly would have stumbled in the darkness had not Mrs. Rose clasped her arm firmly.

"Here we are!" she said, and Dolly saw a large tent, but it wasn't exactly a tent. It was a platform of boards raised not more than a foot above the ground. It had a roof and three sides of canvas, but the front was entirely open. On the floor were piles of balsam boughs and on these the Roses arranged the blankets they had brought.

"I envy you girls," said Mrs. Rose, as she tucked up the impromptu beds. "It is Heavenly to sleep out here, but we older people dare not risk rheumatism. You'll love it, Dolly. Perhaps you'll hear an owl or two hooting you a lullaby."

In less than half an hour the three girls were put to bed and Mrs. Rose had said good-night and left them.

Dotty and Genie had murmured sleepy good-nights and had snuggled down into their spicy-smelling nests of branches.

Dolly lay with wide open eyes staring out at the stars. She had never experienced this sort of thing before, and she was frightened and uncomfortable. Although mid-summer, the air was chilly, and she did not like the feeling of the rather coarse blankets. Moreover she was wearing a thick, clumsy, flannel nightgown, and the bed of branches seemed to be full of knots and lumps. She longed for her own pretty room with its dainty appointments and soft bed clothing.

She looked across at Dotty and Genie. She could see them but dimly, but she knew they were sound asleep. She felt alone, utterly alone in that dreadful place, with the forest trees making a sad murmur and the silent stars winking solemnly at her. She thought of her mother and father and Trudy and Bert and she had the most dreadful wave of homesickness roll over her. Then the tears came, hot, scalding tears that rolled down her cheeks in ever increasing number. She made no noise, lest she waken the other girls but the effort to stifle her sobs made her cry harder, and she buried her face in the rough worsted of the sofa pillow and wiped her eyes with the harsh blanket.

"Oh, Mother," she said, to herself, "I can't stay here. This is a dreadful place. Why did you let me come? I knew I would hate a camp. How can anybody like these awful beds? And I'm cold,—and I'm not cold either, but I'm all shivery and I feel horrid! I'm—I'm— oh, I'm just lonesome and homesick and I want Mother!"

After a time Dolly stopped crying from sheer exhaustion and spent with her sobs, she lay there gazing at the stars. She felt sure there were bears and wolves among the trees, and soon they would come out and attack the camp.

Moreover, she was dreadfully hungry. She had a box of candy in her suitcase, but that was upstairs in the bungalow. She could not get it without disturbing Mr. and Mrs. Rose and that was not to be thought of.

The poor child lay for a time in her misery, every moment

getting more and more homesick and with a deeper longing to get back to her mother and never leave home again.

At last a spirit of desperation took hold upon her. It was characteristic of Dolly Fayre to endure patiently and bravely the greatest trials that might come to her, but when the strain became too great it was in her nature to rebel, suddenly and decidedly.

And now, when it seemed that she simply could not stand the dreadfulness another moment, she sat straight up in bed, and said clearly, "I'm going home."

The sound of her own voice startled her and she looked round quickly to see if the other girls had heard her. She fully expected to see one or both heads pop up in amazement at her speech. But neither dark head moved, and listening to their regular breathing, she knew the two Rose girls were still sound asleep.

With her white face set and a desperate look in her wide open blue eyes, she put one foot out of bed and then the other. She had on her stockings, as Mrs. Rose had advised her to wear them all night. Silently and swiftly she discarded the flannel nightgown, which was one of Dotty's, and with flying fingers, which trembled with a nervous chill, she rapidly dressed herself in the garments she had worn when she arrived.

Her hat and coat were at the bungalow, but she did not stop for them. She was determined to go home that very minute, and she would let nothing interfere.

Fully dressed she went over and looked down at the sleeping Dotty. It seemed awful to go away and leave her like that, but Dolly knew if she waited till morning the Roses would not let her go. And yet she must leave word of some sort or they would think her very rude and ungrateful.

She had with her a little shopping bag, which, as it contained some money, she had put under her pillow. Luckily there was paper and pencil in this on which she had planned to write a letter to her mother.

So with an uncertain hand, in the dim light, she traced the words: "Dear Dotty, I can't stay here, I've got to go back to Mother. Good-bye. Dolly."

This she slipped gently beneath Dotty's pillow, and then stepping softly to the open edge of the tent she stepped down to the ground and walked swiftly toward the lake.

CHAPTER IX

DOLLY'S ESCAPE

Dolly had learned as they came up the lake in the motor boat that there was a footpath along the lake shore which led directly from the camp to the railroad station. It was about a mile long and passed several other camps, but Dolly felt sure that she could walk the distance, and allowing time to rest now and then could reach the station before six o'clock, when the first morning train went through. The dim starlight just enabled her to make out by her little watch that it was two o'clock when she started. She felt no fear of bears or wolves now, for her whole mind and soul were filled with the one idea of going home. She would have started, had the road been lined with hot ploughshares, so indomitable was her will and so strong her resolution. She gave no thought or heed to possible difficulties or dangers. She knew the way, there was no chance of getting lost, and she had in her bag money enough to buy a ticket home. She felt guilty and even ashamed at leaving her kind friends in this manner, but that thought was swallowed up and lost sight of in the terrible gnawing agony of her longing for home.

So she set forth along the path at a swift, steady gait which promised fair for the accomplishment of her design. As she walked along the stars seemed brighter and seemed to wink at her more kindly, as if willing to do all they could to help along a poor little homesick, mother-lonely child. Though without hat or coat, her swift pace kept her warm enough for a time, but at last poor little Dolly grew very weary. She had not walked much since her illness and her newly mended leg felt the strain and began to ache terribly. She sat down to rest on a flat stone and was surprised to find that her leg ached worse sitting down than it had walking. Moreover, when she stopped exercising, she became very chilly and in addition to this she realised afresh that she was exceedingly hungry.

Poor little Dolly! She could scarcely have been more physically miserable, and yet her material discomfort was as nothing to her pangs of homesickness. She felt she could not pursue her journey, and yet it made her shudder to think of returning to that awful camp.

So after a time, hoping she had rested enough, she rose and plodded on again. She kept up this means of procedure, walking until utterly exhausted and then stopping to rest, until somehow she managed to cover the distance to the station.

It was half-past four when she reached the forlorn little building and found it closed and deserted. But there was a bench outside and Dolly sank upon this in a state bordering upon utter collapse. She fell asleep there and was only awakened when, shortly before six, the station agent came to unlock his office.

"Bless my soul! who are you?" he exclaimed, and Dolly sat up blinking in the early sunlight.

"I'm a passenger," she said; "I want to take the early train."

"Humph! a pretty looking passenger you are! Where's your hat?"

"I don't always wear a hat in summer," and Dolly tossed back her golden curls and looked at the man steadily. Her sleep had refreshed her somewhat, and she had recovered her poise. Her determination was still unshaken and she had every intention of going on that six o'clock train.

But the station master was a knowing sort of man and he had before this seen campers afflicted with a desperate desire to go back to civilisation.

"Didn't you come up here last night with the Roses?" he inquired affably.

"Yes," replied Dolly, "but I'm going back to town to-day."

"Pshaw, now, is that so? Don't like it, hey?" The station master had a kindly way with him, and as he threw open the door he invited Dolly to enter the little waiting-room. "You stay here a spell," he said, "that train ain't due for fifteen minutes."

He disappeared into the ticket office and closed the door. Then he called up Mr. Rose on the telephone.

"Hello! what is it?" responded that gentleman sleepily, for he had been roused from a sound slumber.

"I'm Briggs, the station agent. That little yellow-haired girl you brought with you last night is here in the station. Says she's goin' home."

"Dolly Fayre! At the station? Impossible!"

"Yep. She's here. And she's just about all in. You don't want I should let her go on the train, do you?"

"Good gracious, no! Keep her there somehow till I can get there."

"I'll try, but she's terrible set on goin'."

"Keep her somehow, Briggs, if you have to lock her in. I'll be down there inside of half an hour."

"All right, Mr. Rose. Good-bye." Briggs hung up the receiver and sauntered back to the waiting-room.

"Best come over home with me, little Miss and get a bite of

breakfast. How about it? My home's just across the street and my wife'll be glad to give you a snack."

"Thank you," said Dolly, doubtfully, "but I don't want to miss that train."

"Oh, land! she's likely to be half an hour late! Come along, I'll keep my eye out for the train."

Dolly hesitated. She was awfully hungry, but it was five minutes of six and the train might not be late after all. Moreover, it seemed to her that the station man was a little too anxious. Perhaps he wished to detain her, though she could see no reason why he should interfere with her plans. Unless it might be because she had no hat on. Still it was not a crime to go hatless in the summer time, though it might be unconventional when travelling.

"Pretty good breakfast my wife cooks," said Briggs, temptingly.

"Perhaps I would have time just for a glass of milk," said Dolly, "but no, I hear a locomotive whistle now!"

"Aw, she's way up round the bend. Sound carries awful far 'mong these hills. She won't be here for ten minutes yet. Come on."

"What are you talking about? There's the train now!" And from the window Dolly saw the smoke of the approaching engine.

"Why, so 'tis!" and with a strange smile on his face, Briggs whisked the door open, flew out and slammed it behind him and turned the big key, making Dolly a prisoner in the little waiting-room.

For a moment she was too amazed to do or say anything. She stood watching the train draw nearer and stop at the little station.

Then she realised what had happened and she flew to the door and pounded on it with her little fists, crying, "Let me out! you awful, dreadful man, let me out!"

But the door did not open, and after a couple of minutes the train went on its way.

Then Briggs unlocked the door and came in. "Bless my soul!" he said, "if I didn't forget you wanted to go by that train! Well, it's too late now, so you might as well come on over to breakfast."

"You didn't forget it, any such thing! You locked me in here on purpose! You had no right to do it, and my father will pers—persecute you,—or whatever you call it!"

"Well, anyhow the train's gone, and you can't get it back, so make the best of things and smile and come along."

From sheer lack of anything better to do, Dolly rose and walked with Briggs across the street to his little cottage.

"Hello, Mother," he called out, as they entered, "I've brought a visitor to breakfast. Got enough to go round?"

"Yes, indeedy!" and a fat, comfortable looking woman smiled

pleasantly at Dolly; "why, you poor baby, you're all tuckered out. Here sit right down and drink this fresh milk, it's a little warm yet. Take slow sips, now, don't swallow it all at once. Here's a nice piece of toast."

Dolly eagerly accepted the fresh milk and the golden-brown buttered toast, and was glad to follow Mrs. Briggs' advice and partake slowly.

The warm, pleasant room and the appetising food made Dolly feel decidedly better. A poached egg came next and more toast and milk and as both Mr. and Mrs. Briggs were kind and cheery, Dolly's spirits rose accordingly.

No reference was made as to why she wanted to take the train, in fact the subject was not touched on, and Mr. Briggs was entertaining her with a funny story when the door opened and Mr. Rose walked in.

"Hello, Dolly-Polly," he said, cheerily; "had your breakfast? Good for you, Mrs. Briggs, glad you gave the little lady a bite. Come along now, Dolly, we must be on the move."

Mr. Rose's face was so smiling and his manner so pleasant, that Dolly jumped up from her chair and ran to his side. He put his arm round her and kissed her cheek and then with brisk good-byes and thanks to the hospitable Briggs, he whisked Dolly away.

"Skip it!" he said, and taking her hand they skipped across the road and down the long length of the pier. There was Mr. Rose's motor-boat waiting, with Long Sam at the wheel.

"Mornin' folkses," he said, unfolding his ungainly length as he rose to help them in. Long Sam, it was generally agreed, had the longest length for the narrowest width of any man in the county. He grinned at Dolly and taking her hands helped her into the boat, while Mr. Rose followed.

In a moment they were off, and the little boat scooted up the lake in a hurry. The sun was well up now and it was a warm day, so the lake breeze was most refreshing and the swift motion very exhilarating. Mr. Rose said no word whatever concerning Dolly's informal departure from his camp, but he was so gay and entertaining that Dolly herself forgot it. He pointed out various houses and camps along the shore, often telling funny stories of the people who lived there. He showed her the club house and the casino and the picnic grounds and lots of interesting places, which had passed unnoticed on their trip up the lake the night before. Sometimes Long Sam put in a few words in his dry, comical way, and Dolly found herself enjoying the morning lake ride immensely.

Mr. Rose was in the midst of a funny story at which Dolly was shaking with laughter as they reached the pier which belonged to Crosstrees camp.

"Out you hop!" exclaimed Mr. Rose, jumping out himself and in a moment Dolly was beside him on the pier. Mrs. Rose and the two girls stood there smiling, their arms full of bathing suits.

"Hurry up, Doll," cried Dotty, grabbing her arm. "This is your bathhouse right next to mine and here's your suit. Scrabble into it, quick's you can."

And so almost before she knew it, Dolly was shut in to her little bath house and was hastily changing from her street suit to her bathing-dress.

Just as she finished arraying herself, Dotty was pounding on the door and she immediately opened it. Mrs. Rose put a bathing cap on Dolly's head and tied a gay kerchief over that. The rest were all in bathing suits and with gay laughter they all joined hands and ran down the sloping shore and into the lake.

Dolly loved bathing and she pranced round with the rest, enjoying the delightful feel of the cool ripples of the lake as they dashed against her.

The young people were not allowed to go out very far alone, but Mr. Rose would swim out with them, one at a time, for a short distance and return them safely to shallower water.

"Do teach me to swim," pleaded Dolly, who took to water like a duck. So Mr. Rose gave her her first lesson and she was so promising a pupil that he declared she would soon learn to become expert.

The bath over, they returned to the bath houses to dress and Dolly found in hers, instead of her travelling suit, a serge skirt and middy blouse. She put these on, and when she went out she found Dotty similarly arrayed. Mrs. Rose braided the two girls' hair in long pig-tails and tied their ribbons for them.

"Now for a camp breakfast!" exclaimed Mr. Rose, as the group reunited.

"I've had my breakfast," began Dolly, but Mr. Rose interrupted her, saying, "indeed you haven't! Just wait till you see."

In a little clearing not far from the bungalow, Dolly saw a table of boards with seats each side and here the family gathered.

Such a breakfast as it was! Maria's flap-jacks had materialised and of all light, puffy, golden delicacies they were the best. Then there was brook trout, fresh and delicious; a tempting omelet; and as a great treat the girls were each allowed a cup of coffee.

The trip up the lake and the invigorating bath had given Dolly a ravenous appetite and never had food tasted so good. She didn't quite understand why nothing was said about her running away in the night, but it was a great relief that the subject was not touched upon, and in the gay laughter and chatter of the Rose family, she finally forgot all about it.

"Now, who's for a tramp in the woods?" and Mr. Rose lighted a cigar as he left the table.

"Me!" cried Dolly, dancing up to her host; "when can we start?"

"Right away quick," and Mr. Rose smiled down at her; "have you good stout shoes?"

"Yes, indeed," and Dolly showed her little tan boots.

The whole family started off, each with a stout stick to help their steps in climbing, and each with a little basket, because, as Mr. Rose said, "you never can tell what you'll find to bring home."

They started off briskly, Dolly and Dotty on either side of Mr. Rose and Genie and her mother following close behind.

"Guess we'll try the Rocky Chasm path this morning," said Mr. Rose, who acted as guide.

Away they went, walking briskly, but not too rapidly. Though it was a warm day the path through the woods was cool and pleasant and occasionally they paused to rest for a time. Presently the climbing began and this they took by easy stages, so that when at last they reached their goal, Dolly was not at all tired.

"What a beautiful place!" she cried, as they found themselves on top of a high hill looking down into a rocky chasm.

"Don't go too near the edge," warned Mrs. Rose as her husband and the two girls went to peer over the edge of the precipice.

"No, indeed!" he returned, "but Dolly must see down in the chasm. Here, Dot, you show her how."

So Dotty lay down flat on the rocks and wriggled along until she could see over the very edge while her father held tightly to her feet.

"It's wonderful!" she exclaimed; "now you try it, Dolly."

Somewhat timidly, but with full faith in Mr. Rose, Dolly lay down prone, and cautiously edged along till she could see over the shelving rock. She felt Mr. Rose's firm grip on her ankles, and she looked down with wonder at the sheer straight descent of rock and down at the very bottom of the chasm she saw a tiny brook tossing and foaming along.

"Not yet!" she called as Mr. Rose advised her to come back. "Let me see it a moment longer!"

"Don't get dizzy!" called out Mrs. Rose.

"No, indeed!" said Dolly, as at last Mr. Rose pulled her in; "I wasn't dizzy a bit! I never saw anything so wonderful. That beautiful little brook way down there a thousand miles below!"

"Oh, not quite so far as that," said Mr. Rose, laughing. "Come on; let's go down and see it from below."

They picked up their baskets and following Mr. Rose's direction they climbed down a rocky ravine and, sure enough, found themselves right beside the little tumbling brook. Dolly sat on a rock and gazed upward at the precipice, looking at the very spot where she had poked her head over.

"Were we really up there looking down?" she exclaimed. "I can hardly believe it. Oh, what a lovely place this is!"

"Yes, isn't it!" cried Dotty; "let's dig something, Daddy."

"What can we find?" And Mr. Rose looked around. "Why, my goodness, my basket is full already!"

"What's in it?" cried Genie, scampering around to see. "Oh, goody! cookies and lemonade!"

Though Dolly had really had two breakfasts, the mountain climb had made her ready to welcome a little light refreshment and the bottles of lemonade and the box of cookies were rapidly disposed of by the party.

"I see Indian Pipes," remarked Mr. Rose, and Dotty cried, "Where? Where?"

"Those who seek will find," said Mr. Rose, smiling, and the girls set to work hunting.

Dotty was the first to spy some of the graceful white blossoms under some concealing green leaves, but a moment later Dolly found some too. With their trowels they carefully dug up the plants and put them in their baskets to take home.

Genie collected some odd stones, and Mrs. Rose found a particular bit of Eglantine that she wanted and soon the baskets were filled and the party took up their homeward way.

Mostly of a down-hill trend, the way home was easy, and as the baskets were not heavy the girls danced gaily along singing songs as they went.

"Why, goodness, gracious sakes; it's nearly two o'clock!" cried Dolly as they entered the big living room of the bungalow and set down their burdens.

"It sho'ly is!" and Maria's black face appeared in the doorway. "I suttinly thought you-all was never comin' home to dinner! I'se been waitin' and waitin' till everything is jes' 'bout spoilt!"

"Oh, I guess not as bad as that, Maria," and Mr. Rose smiled pleasantly at her. "We're not much behind time, and we won't grumble if things are cold."

"Laws' sakes! they ain't cold! I'se dun looked out for dat. Yo' better wash that mud off your hands and come along. Doan' waste no time now."

The Roses were accustomed to Maria's good-natured scoldings and they ran away to follow her advice.

CHAPTER X

HIDDEN TREASURE

"Take time to tidy up and put on clean blouses," called out Mrs. Rose as the girls went to their rooms.

But they made quick work of it, and helped each other in the matter of hair ribbons and soon three very trim and tidy young persons in clean white linen presented themselves, hungry for their dinner.

Maria had a steaming chicken stew for them, with fluffy white dumplings that showed no sign of being "spoilt"; in fact, she had not cooked them until after the family's return.

"Was there ever anything so good!" exclaimed Dolly as she received a second portion of the fricassee.

"Everything tastes good up here," said Dotty, "but Maria sure is a dandy on stewed chicken. But go easy, Doll, for I happen to know there's an Apple Betty to follow and just you wait till you see that!"

But Dolly's camp appetite was quite equal to the Apple Betty also, which was, as Dolly had predicted, a triumph in the matter of desserts.

"I feel as if I had been to a party," Dolly said as they left the table. "I believe I've eaten more to-day than I do in a week at home."

"It's the air," said Mr. Rose. "Crosstrees' air is the greatest appetiser known to man. If I could bottle it and sell it, I'd make my everlasting fortune. Now, may I ask what you young ladies have on hand for this afternoon?"

"Nothing particular," said Dotty. "Why?"

"Because I asked a few young people from the neighbouring camps to come over here for awhile."

"A party?" cried Genie. "Oh, Daddy, a party?"

"Not exactly a party; only half a dozen of the Norrises and Holmeses."

"Lovely!" cried Dotty. "I haven't seen the Norrises since last year, and I don't know the Holmeses. Who are they?"

"Mr. Holmes is a friend of mine and his daughter Edith is about the age of you girls, and they have two or three guests."

"And the Norrises, Maisie and Jack, are awfully nice," said Dotty. "You'll like them, Doll; Maisie is something like you."

"She isn't a bit like Dolly," put in Genie, "'cept she's fat and yellow headed and blue eyed. But she isn't half as pretty as Dolly, so don't you mind, Dollyrinda."

66

"Oh, I don't mind," and Dolly laughed. "I don't think a blue-eyed Towhead can be pretty anyway. I like dark eyes and dark curls best."

"Thank you, ma'am," and Dotty dropped a curtsey. "Shall we dress up, Mother?"

"No; those clean blouses are all right. It's just a camp frolic, not a formal party."

"It's a Kidd party," observed Mr. Rose, looking mysterious.

"A kid party?" echoed Dotty; "of course. I didn't s'pose it was a grown-up party, Daddy, for us children."

Mr. Rose only laughed and turned away, and the girls wandered out toward the open tent where Dolly had gone to bed the night before.

The hemlock-bough beds were covered now with big spreads of gay cretonne and many cretonne pillows, and served as day couches.

The sight of the tent recalled to Dolly's mind the events of the night before, and she suddenly experienced a wave of embarrassment and remorse at the way she had acted. She felt, too, that an apology was due to her hosts and somehow it didn't seem right to talk about it to the girls for she felt that it was to Mr. and Mrs. Rose she owed an explanation.

"Wait here for me a minute," she said suddenly to Dolly and Genie, and turning, she ran back to the bungalow.

She found Mr. and Mrs. Rose in the living room, and going straight to them she said impulsively, "I was very naughty to run away last night and I want to apologise. You see I got homesick—"

"Bless your heart; don't say a word about it," said Mr. Rose, in the kindest tones; "that's part of the performance, child. Everybody gets homesick the first night in camp. It's to be expected. Then, you see, the next day they begin to like it and the third day you couldn't drive them home."

"But I was very impolite to go away like that—"

"Never mind, Dollikins," and Mrs. Rose put her arm around her little visitor; "it's all right, dearie; don't think of it again. I know perfectly well how forlorn you felt and how you wanted your mother. And I know, too, you were chilly and you felt strange and lonesome and couldn't sleep. But that's all over now and we won't even think of it again. If you don't sleep all right to-night and if you want to go home to-morrow, I'll take you down myself, right straight to where your mother is. Now put it all out of your mind and scamper back to Dotty. The party will be coming pretty soon now."

"Run along," and Mr. Rose patted the golden head. "You wouldn't have been the right kind of a guest at all if you hadn't been

67

homesick the first night. But I'll bet you a ripe red apple that you won't want to go home to-morrow, but if you do want to you shall. Now skip along, for if I'm not mistaken I hear a motor boat and like as not it's that bunch from the Holmes'."

Dolly ran away, her heart greatly lightened by the kind attitude of her hosts, and though she felt sorry she had run away the night before, she did not feel so ashamed since they had so pleasantly made light of it.

Sure enough, the party of young people were just coming along the pier, and Edith Holmes, a bright girl of about Dolly's age, was introducing herself and her friends.

"I'm Edith Holmes," she said, laughing, "and these are my cousins, Guy and Elmer. They're nice enough boys, but here's their sister Josie who is nicer yet."

Josie was a shy little thing, who blushed and cast down her eyes at Edith's praise.

"I thought the Norrises would be here," went on Edith, "and as they know us and know you they could introduce us better. But we'll just scrape acquaintance."

"Oh, that's all right," said Dotty. "I'm Dotty Rose and this is my chum, Dolly Fayre, and my little sister, Genie. I have a brother but he isn't here." She smiled at the boys as she said this and Elmer Holmes said, "That doesn't matter; we just love to play with girls. And anyhow here comes Jack Norris to keep us in countenance."

Jack and Maisie Norris came along, having walked over from the next camp. They were acquainted with the Holmes' young people as both families had been there all summer.

Introductions over, they all sat along the edge of the open tent. The floor of this, being only about a foot above ground, made a convenient seat and those who wished had cushions to sit on or lean against.

"Awful glad you people got up here at last," said Maisie Norris as she twisted one of Dotty's curls round her finger. "Is your arm all well, Dot?"

"Yes, though it isn't awfully strong yet. I have to be a little careful. But it was my left one, you know, so I can play croquet and tennis and do most everything."

"You had a gay old mixup, didn't you?" said Jack Norris, smiling at Dolly. "You broke yourself, too, didn't you?"

"Oh, yes; you know Dotty and I are next-door neighbours this year, and whatever one of us does the other has to. But we're both mended now and ready for any sort of fun."

Then Mr. Rose came along, bringing about a dozen spades.

They were small ones, such as come with children's gardening tools, and he gave one to each of the young people present.

"What for?" asked Elmer Holmes, as he looked at the shining new tool.

"I told my girls that this was to be a Kidd party," said Mr. Rose, "but they didn't quite understand what I meant. Now I'll explain. Has each one a spade?"

"Yes," and the nine boys and girls held them up.

"All right then. Now, what you want to do is to dig for Captain Kidd's buried treasure. You have all heard that old Captain Kidd buried a lot of treasure somewhere, but I doubt if you were aware that he buried it in Crosstrees Camp. However, there is a tradition to that effect and so I would like you to do your best to find it. Tradition says that the treasure was buried somewhere near the spot where we are now. It is hidden, I believe, not farther than fifty feet away in any direction from this open tent, so everybody may dig wherever he chooses within that radius, and see if he can unearth the treasure."

"But, Daddy," said Genie, "how do we know where to dig?"

"That you must decide for yourselves. Dig any place you like; turn up the whole area if you choose; or, if you see a place that seems especially hopeful, dig there. I feel sure the treasure is really buried somewhere around and it's up to you young people to discover where it may be."

"We'll find it!" and Jack Norris brandished his spade in the air. "Come on, girls and boys; let's dig down to China if necessary, but let's get Kidd's old treasure chest."

The young people scattered, looking about for probable places to dig.

Dolly, a little unused to digging, began rather aimlessly to toss up the soil near by where she stood.

"Oh, I say," said Jack Norris, "don't start in that way. Come along with me and let's find a place that looks promising."

They walked away, looking eagerly at the ground about them, when Dolly spied something white under the leaves of a vine.

"Oh, look here!" she cried, and Jack stooped down to see what it was. They saw a grinning skull and cross bones made of white plaster and partly sunken in the earth.

"Geewhillikens! we've struck it!" cried Jack, "or rather you have! I felt sure from that twinkle in Mr. Rose's eye that there was some way of knowing where to dig. This is it, of course. The treasure is buried here! Let's dig for it!"

Carefully setting aside the little skull, which was only a papier-maché toy, they both began to dig desperately.

69

"The ground is soft! It has lately been dug, you see, to plant the box here. How lucky you saw that white thing under the leaves."

"You would have seen it if I hadn't," said Dolly, not wanting to take all the credit to herself. "It's buried pretty deep, isn't it?"

"Yes, sort of. Don't you dig any more, if you're tired; I'll dig the rest of the way."

Dolly paused a few moments, and Jack went on digging. At last he said, as he straightened himself up and wiped his brow with his handkerchief, "Do you know, I believe we're hoaxed! I believe that skull was there to fool us!"

"Oh, I'll bet it was!" and Dolly's eyes danced as she realised the situation. "Maybe there are other skulls in other places!"

"I shouldn't wonder. Let's go and see."

"Let's fill up this hole first and put the skull back to fool somebody else."

"All right," and Jack hastily tossed the dirt back into the hole, and replaced the little white skull.

"Somebody is coming this way! Let's hide," and Dolly and Jack quickly whisked themselves behind a clump of trees.

Guy Holmes and Maisie Norris came along and they spied the white skull which Jack had left placed rather more conspicuously than he had found it.

"Oh, look at that!" cried Guy, and Maisie exclaimed, "This is the right place, of course! We've struck it at last! That pirate flag was just to fool us. Hooray! let's dig!"

Dolly and Jack could scarcely keep from laughing aloud as they saw the newcomers digging desperately in the very spot they had dug themselves.

At last Jack beckoned to Dolly and they softly glided away without letting the others know of their presence.

"Now we want to find where it really is," whispered Jack as soon as they were out of hearing of the others. "I say, this is a great game! and we've learned something from those people. The spot marked with a pirate flag is not the right one! When we find that, there is no use of digging."

The pair went on, prospecting for a likely place to dig. There were so many trees and shrubs, that often there would be no view of any of the other seekers. And then again they would come across groups of two or three, or perhaps one alone digging desperately or looking disappointed at a failure.

Gay greetings were exchanged or words of sympathy and commiseration and each went on his chosen way.

"Do you know," said Jack at last, "I shouldn't be surprised if the real place isn't marked at all. Hullo, what's this?" Right at his feet lay a toy bowie-knife. Though made of pasteboard, it was a ferocious-looking affair and the spot where it was had not been disturbed.

"I don't believe that's the right place," said Jack, who had grown suspicious of misleading clues. "Anyway, Dolly, let's leave that, and come back to it if we don't find anything more hopeful."

So they wandered on and next they came to the pirate flag. This black and white emblem was planted above a much dug up space and they laughed as they concluded that several trials had been made there.

Soon they came upon Dotty and Josie Holmes who were hastily digging at a spot which had been marked by two stakes. They had pulled up the stakes, but as yet had not found any treasure.

"Bet it isn't there," said Jack, looking closely at the two stakes.

"Why?" demanded Dotty.

"Dunno. Somehow it doesn't seem 'sif it is. Come on, Dolly, let's try again."

"Go on," said Dotty; "I think this is the place. Josie and I feel certain of it. Go on, you two, and good luck to you."

Shouldering their spades, Jack and Dolly trudged on.

"Let's think it out," said Jack, seating himself on a flat rock, while Dolly did likewise. "I believe we can think out where Mr. Rose would have been likely to put the thing. Now I don't believe it would be very close to where he started us. These nearby digging places are all frauds. Let's go to the limit of the space he said, and try all 'round the edge."

"How can you tell?" And Dolly looked at him with a puzzled expression.

"Why, he said fifty feet, you know, and I can pace off what ought to be about fifty feet and then we'll walk all the way round."

They did this, and as they walked round the circle which Jack declared was about the boundary of the fifty-foot radius, they soon came upon a good-sized iron key.

"This is it!" cried Jack; "we've struck it! This is the key to the chest, and the chest is buried here!"

"Good work!" and Guy Holmes and Maisie Norris appeared just in time to hear Jack's exclamation. "Come on, let's all dig!"

"No," said Dolly, sitting down on the ground; "I can't dig any more; I'm too tired. Maisie and I will sit here while you boys do the digging."

"All right," the boys agreed, and they fell to work with a will.

They had thrown out but a few spadefulls of dirt, when they struck something hard.

71

"Hooray! hurroo!" cried Guy; "we've got it! We've struck the treasure!"

"Sure we have!" and Jack flung out the dirt excitedly. "Easy there now, old fellow! Look out! It's the chest, sure enough!"

The two girls jumped up and ran to look, as the boys uncovered one corner of what seemed to be an old brass-bound chest.

"It is; it is!" cried Dolly. "We've found it. Hooray, everybody! We've found the treasure!"

As her voice rang out the others left their digging and all congregated about the lucky finders.

Other spades were set to work and in a short time willing hands lifted the old chest from the hole and set it up on the solid earth.

"It's locked!" cried somebody, as several tried to open it at once.

"Of course it is," said Dolly; "don't you remember, Jack, it was the key that first showed us where it was. What did you do with that key?"

"I don't know," and Jack Norris began looking around.

"I know," said Dolly, laughing; "you left it on the ground and you spaded out the dirt all over it. Now you'll have to dig for the key!"

"That's just what I did do! If I'm not the chump!" and Jack began to dig in the heap of dirt they had thrown up out of the hole.

"Toss it back in the hole," cried Guy, and in a jiffy the dirt was flung back where it came from and the key was discovered.

"Don't let's open the box here," said Dolly; "I think we ought to take it to Mr. Rose first."

"I think so, too," agreed Jack Norris, and the boys carried the big box, while Dolly and the girls followed with the key.

"Here you are, Captain Kidd," cried Jack as they met Mr. Rose already coming to meet them.

"Found it, did you?" said that gentleman, smiling at the band of treasure seekers. "Bring it along and we'll open it."

They all followed him to the bungalow veranda, and there the treasure chest was unlocked.

It contained a little souvenir for everybody present and there were exclamations of delight over the pretty trinkets that were found tied up in dainty tissue paper parcels that did not look at all as if they had been prepared by Captain Kidd or his pirate crew!

Dolly's gift was a pretty writing tablet, well furnished, and upon which, she declared, she should write a long letter home telling of the treasure hunt and its success.

Later on a jolly picnic supper was served to the young people and before this was finished the sun had set and the stars were beginning to show above the tall trees.

"Now for a real camp-fire," said Mr. Rose, leading the way to the open tent. "Come on, boys, and help me fetch wood."

The boys followed their host and under direction of Mrs. Rose and Dotty the open tent was transformed into a cosy and inviting place. Hemlock and spruce boughs were thrown about and partly covered with Indian blankets and many cushions and pillows and mats of woven rattan.

Mrs. Rose and the girls arranged themselves comfortably in this spicy nest and when the boys returned with arms full of fagots and brush, Mr. Rose superintended the building of a glorious fire right in front of the open tent.

Then the party all gathered together and sang songs and told stories and cracked jokes in merry mood.

The blazing fire cast grotesque shadows all about and the merry crackling blaze was a joy of itself.

Boxes of marshmallows made their appearance and faces took on a rosy glow as the young people toasted the white lumps of delight on the ends of long forks provided by Maria.

"I never had such a good time in my life," exclaimed Dolly, her eyes dancing and her cheeks rosy as she scampered around the fire.

"Do you like camping?" asked Jack Norris, looking admiringly at the pretty laughing face.

"I just love it!" Dolly cried, and everybody wondered why all the Rose family chuckled with glee.

"Haven't you ever been up here before?" asked Jack.

"No; I never saw a camp-fire before. I had no idea these things were such fun. This has been the most beautiful day in my life!" And Dolly looked roguishly up into the face of Mr. Rose who chanced to be passing by. "And I thank you for it," she added, slipping her hand into his.

Mr. Rose gave her little hand a warm welcoming grasp as he answered, "I'm awfully glad you're enjoying it and you are very welcome to Camp Crosstrees!"

CHAPTER XI

A THRILLING EXPERIENCE

After that the days just fairly flew. Dolly changed her mind completely and concluded that camp life was one of the jolliest things in the world.

Talking things over with Dotty, she explained her lonesomeness and homesickness that first night.

"Yes, I understand," and Dotty wagged her head sagaciously. "Most everybody doesn't like camp at first and we didn't have any fun that first night, but, you see, we all knew the fun was coming next days and you didn't."

"It was partly that," said Dolly, honestly, "and partly 'cause I felt that I must see Mother. You see, I've never been away from her all night before, and it was so queer sleeping outdoors, and I was sort of cold, and—"

"I know! You were hungry! There's nothing makes anybody as homesick as being hungry. Supper was skinny that night, I remember, and I was hungry too, only I went to sleep and forgot all about it. Come on, Doll, let's go over to the Norrises."

"All right," and having informed Mrs. Rose of their intention the two girls set off for the Norris camp, which was but a short distance away.

To their disappointment, when they reached there, they learned that Mrs. Norris had taken both Maisie and Jack to town with her to do some shopping, and they would not be back before six o'clock.

It was Sarah, the nurse girl, who told them this, as she sat on the verandah taking care of Gladys, the two-year-old Norris baby.

"Let's stay a few minutes and play with the kiddy," said Dolly, patting the little fat hand of the smiling child.

"All right," agreed Dotty; "let's take her in the swing."

The two girls with Gladys between them sat in the wide porch swing and Sarah said diffidently, "Would you two young ladies mind keeping the baby for half an hour, while I run down the road a piece to see my sister? She's awful sick."

"Go ahead, Sarah," said Dolly, good-naturedly. "We'll take care of Gladys. She won't cry, will she?"

"That she won't. She's the best baby in the world. There's a couple of crackers you can give her if she's hungry, or the cook will give you a cup of milk for her. I won't be gone long."

"Don't stay more than half an hour, Sarah," said Dotty; "I'd just as lieve keep the baby but I don't know as Mrs. Norris would like it to have you go away from the child."

"Oh, pshaw!" said Dolly; "the baby is all right with us. Stay as long as you want to, Sarah; I just love to take care of babies."

So Sarah went away and the two girls proceeded to give Gladys the time of her life. They soon tired of the swing and took the baby out into the woods, where they crowned her with leaves and called her Queen of the May.

The child laughed and crowed, and as her language was limited she called both the girls Doddy, and beamed on them both impartially. Herself she called Daddy, being unable to achieve her own name.

"Two Doddies take Daddy saily-bye!" she cried, waving her fat hands toward the lake.

"Oh, no," said Dolly; "Daddy go saily-bye when Jack comes home."

"No! no wait for Dak! Daddy 'ant to go saily now! Daddy go in boat! Two Doddy go in boat and sail Daddy far, far away!" The two little arms waved as if indicating a journey round the world, and the baby face beamed so coaxingly that Dolly couldn't resist it.

"We'll go down to the shore," she said, "and Gladys can paddle her hands in the water; that will be nice."

"Ess!" and the baby danced with glee as the three went down to the lake.

There was a short bit of fairly good beach at the Norrises' place, and here the children sat down to play. A sail boat, a row boat and a canoe were tied there and soon Gladys renewed her plea to go sailing.

The girls tried to divert her mind, for they were not willing to take the responsibility of taking the little girl out on the water.

"Maybe we might take her out in the row boat," suggested Dotty, but Dolly said, "No, I'd rather not. I can row well enough, but you can't do much with your weak arm and suppose anything should happen to this blessed child! No, siree, Dot; I'm not going to take any such risk."

"I think you're silly. We could row around near shore and it would please the baby a heap. She's going to cry if you don't."

Dotty's prediction seemed in imminent danger of being fulfilled, but Dolly sprang up and began a frolicking song and dance intended to divert the baby's attention.

But for a few moments only Gladys was pleased with this entertainment. With the persistency of her kind, she returned again and again to the subject of her greatly desired water trip.

Still being denied, she set up a first class crying act. It scarcely seemed possible that so many tears could come from those two blue eyes! She didn't scream or howl, but she cried desperately, continuously, and with heartbroken sobs until the two caretakers were filled with consternation.

No effort to divert her was successful. In no game or play would she show any interest, and as the little face grew red from the continued sobbing, Dotty exclaimed, "That child will have a fit, if she doesn't get what she wants! Now look here, Doll; we won't go in a boat, but let's put the baby in the canoe and just pull her back and forth gently by the rope. It's tied fast to the post."

Dolly looked doubtful, but as the baby sensed Dotty's words a heavenly smile broke over her face and she exclaimed, "Ess, ess! Daddy go saily-bye all aloney!"

Dolly still hesitated, but Dotty picked up the eager child and plumped her down in the middle of the canoe, which was partly drawn up on the shelving beach. A little push set it afloat and grasping the rope firmly, Dotty gently pushed and pulled the canoe back and forth, while the baby squealed with delight.

"That can't do any harm," said Dotty, pleased with the success of her scheme, and Dolly agreed that Gladys was safe enough as long as she sat still.

"Even if she should spill out, she'd only get wet," said Dotty; "the water isn't six inches deep where she is. And you will sit still, won't you, baby?"

"Ess, Daddy sit still," and the baby folded her hands and sat motionless in the canoe, only swaying slightly with the motion as Dotty slowly pulled her in shore and then let her drift back again.

"It's like a new-fashioned cradle," said Dolly; "I'll hold the rope for awhile, Dot."

"All right, take it; it hurts your hand a little after awhile."

So Dolly pulled the rope and the two girls sitting on the beach chatted away while the baby floated back and forth.

"Let me take it now," said Dotty after a time; "you must be tired."

"No, I'm not a bit tired, and I can use two hands while you can use only one. You oughtn't to use that left flapper of yours much while it's weak, Dot."

"Pooh, it isn't weak! It's as strong as anything. Give me that rope!"

"No, sir, I won't do it," and there was a good-natured scuffle for the possession of the rope as the four hands grabbed at it and each pair tried to get the other pair off.

"Let go, you!" cried Dotty, pulling at Dolly's hands.

"Let go yourself!" Dolly replied, laughingly, and then,—they never knew quite how it happened, but somehow their scramble had pulled the rope loose from the post, and as they twisted each other's hands, the rope slipped away from them and slid away under the water.

The lake was full of cross currents and even before they realised what had happened the canoe was several feet from shore. To Gladys it seemed like some new game and she clapped her hands and shouted in glee, "Daddy saily all aloney,—far, far away!" She waved her baby arms and rocked back and forth in joy.

Dotty and Dolly were for a moment paralysed with fright. Then Dotty, grabbing Dolly's arm, said, "Don't stand there like that! We must do something! That baby will drown! Let's holler for help."

Dotty tried to scream, but her heart was beating so wildly and her nerves pulsing so rapidly she could make scarcely any sound, and her wail of agony died away in a whisper.

"I can't yell, either," said Dolly, hoarsely, as she trembled like a leaf. "But we must do something! Don't go to pieces, Dotty—"

"Go to pieces nothing! You're going to faint yourself. Now stop it, Dollyrinda," and Dotty gave her a shake. "We've got to save that child, no matter how we do it!— Sit still, baby, won't you?" she called to Gladys.

But the child bounced about in her new-found freedom and grasping each side of the canoe with her little hands began to rock it as hard as her baby strength would allow.

"Oh!" breathed Dolly, who was watching with staring eyes; "sit still, little Gladys; don't rock the boat, dearie."

"Ess; rock-a-by-baby, in a saily boat!" and again Gladys swayed the little craft from side to side.

"We must make her stop that first of all," and Dotty wrung her hands as she stepped down to the water's edge and even into the water as she called to the baby. "Gladys, sit very still, and Doddy come out there in another boat. Sit very still."

Gladys did sit still, and the canoe floated steadily on the smooth lake. But it drifted farther and farther from land and now about twenty feet of water separated the baby from the shore.

"We've got to get in the row boat and go out there," said Dotty, who was already untying the rope.

"Yes, it's the only thing to do," agreed Dolly; "but you can't row, Dot, and I can. So I'll take the boat, and you run for help. I don't know whether you'd better go to the Norrises; I don't think there's anybody there but the cook, or whether you'd better make straight for home and get your father to come."

"I'll do both! I can run, if I can't row!" and Dotty flew off like a deer up the hill toward the Norris camp.

Dolly stepped into the boat and shipped the oars. It was a large flat-bottomed boat and the oars were heavy. Dolly knew how to row but she was not expert at it, and, too, she dreaded to turn around with her back to the baby. "Though," she thought to herself, in an agony of conflicting ideas, "I've got to row out there, and I can't do it and keep watch of Gladys both."

She pulled a few strokes, twisting her head between each to get a glimpse of the baby who was now sitting quietly in the canoe, drifting out toward the middle of the lake.

Not a motor boat or craft of any kind that might lend assistance was in sight. They were at the extreme upper end of the lake and most of the camps were farther down. Vainly Dolly scanned the water for a boat of any kind, but saw none. Bravely she pulled at the big oars, but she was not an athletic girl, and having been laid up so long with a broken leg her muscles were weak.

She pulled as hard as she could, in a straight line toward the canoe, but though she succeeded in lessening the distance between them she could not get very near the baby, for the canoe drifted steadily away.

At last, by almost superhuman efforts, she came within a few feet of the child, and then fearing to bump into the canoe and upset it, she turned around and tried to back water gently. But the big oars were ungainly and the task was not easy.

Moreover, Gladys was overjoyed at seeing Dolly in the other boat and she expressed her joy by leaning over the side of the canoe.

Dolly's heart seemed to stop beating as she saw the wobbly little boat career with the laughing baby leaning far over the edge. She knew she must not alarm the child and so in a desperate endeavour to speak naturally, she called out, "Sit up straight, baby; see how straight you can sit!"

"So straight!" and Gladys emphasised her straightness by putting both arms up in the air.

"Yes, dear. Now fold your arms and sit straight."

Gladys obeyed and folded her chubby arms and sat motionless right in the middle of the canoe.

Dolly's heart bounded with thankfulness as with aching arms she pushed her way nearer the drifting canoe. She was moving stern first and tried to manœuvre to try to come up sideways against the canoe. Then if she could lift the baby safely into her own flat-bottomed boat she would be content to drift about until help came.

How many times she tried! But just as her boat would near the other, a chance current or a puff of wind would take the canoe just out of her reach. Paddling now with one oar she came very near the unsteady little craft, so near that Gladys suddenly decided to jump into Dolly's boat.

The child scrambled to her knees and leaned over the side of the canoe till she was almost in the water.

"Sit down!" screamed Dolly frantically, forgetting the danger of suddenness.

Gladys was startled and instead of sitting down leaned farther over the edge, and the canoe capsized!

Dolly's face blanched, her oars dropped from her hands and every muscle in her body went limp. Then the impulse came to jump in the water after the child. Seizing the row-lock, she was about to plunge, blindly, heedlessly, but obeying the irresistible impulse, when something white appeared on the water, right at her very side. It was Gladys's white dress, and Dolly made a grab for it just as it was again about to sink from sight.

She held on firmly, though it seemed as if her strength was ebbing rapidly away.

She strove with all her might to pull the baby into her own boat, but she could not lift the heavy child over the edge. How glad she was now that she was in the big flat-bottomed boat, which was in little if any danger of upsetting.

Not knowing whether the baby was dead or alive, she hung on to the precious burden, still trying to lift her over the edge, but unable to do so. It was all she could do to keep her grasp on the wet clothing and keep the child's head above water as the eddies tossed her boat around on the rough surface of the lake. The waves were choppy and every time she would nearly succeed in lifting the baby in, a sudden lurch would almost make her lose her grip.

It was when at last she almost felt the little form slipping from her grasp that she heard the chug-chug of a motor boat and a cheery, loud voice sang out, "Hang on, Dolly; hang on! All right, we're coming!"

Dolly didn't dare look up, but with her last ounce of strength she hung on to the baby's white dress, which she had already torn to ribbons in her clutches. She heard the swift oncoming of the motor boat and feared lest its waves might even yet wash the little form away that she held so insecurely. She refused to lift her eyes as the sound of the engine grew louder and she felt a sickening fear of the first waves that might reach her from the motor boat.

To her dismay she felt her hold loosening. Her muscles were powerless longer to stand the strain of the baby's weight. She heard the motor and she felt, or imagined she did, the first of the rhythmic waves that would, she felt certain, as they grew stronger, tear the child from her grasp. In desperation she bunched up a portion of the little white dress and leaning her head down clinched it firmly in her teeth.

But even as she did so, she knew she could not hold it there. The wet cloth choked her, and the water dashed in her face and blinded her. A sickening conviction came to her that it was all over and in another instant little Gladys would fall away from her helpless hands, and drown.

But to her ears there came a sound of a human voice. Not a shout, not even a loud call, but a calm, pleasant voice close to her, that said: "All right Dolly! Let go. You have saved Gladys!"

Mechanically obeying, though scarcely knowing what she did, Dolly opened her teeth and as the baby slid from her numbed fingers the child was grasped by strong arms, and Mr. Rose's face appeared to Dolly's view. He had swum from the motor boat, and now holding Gladys in one arm he hung on to the row boat with the other.

"Take her in," he said, as he lifted the child over the edge into the boat.

The reaction brought back Dolly's lost nerve. Gladly she received the little form in her arms and in another moment Mr. Rose had himself scrambled, big and dripping, into the boat also.

"You little trump!" he exclaimed; "you brick! you heroine! Let me take the baby. Why, she's all right!"

Gladys, though she had been partly unconscious, while in the water, was really unharmed and as Mr. Rose held her to him she opened her eyes and smiled.

Swiftly the motor boat came and took the three on board, and dragging the row boat behind them, they made quickly for the shore.

"Well, I swan!" exclaimed Long Sam, who was at the wheel, "if you Dolly ain't the rippenest little mortal! However you managed to keep a grip on that there kid is more'n I can tell!"

"I'm sure I can't tell you," and Dolly smiled, out of sheer happiness at Gladys' safety.

They reached the shore in a few moments and Mrs. Rose was there with a big blanket in which to wrap the baby while they carried her up to the house. Sarah the nurse was there, and soon Gladys, warmed and fed and arrayed in dry clothes, was pronounced by all to be none the worse for her thrilling experience.

Dolly, however, was exhausted. Mrs. Rose, after leaving the baby to the nurse, hurried Dolly home and put her to bed.

"Yes, my dear," she said as Dolly objected; "you have an ordeal to go through with as heroine of this occasion. When Mrs. Norris comes home, she will come over here to give you a medal for bravery and heroism and general life-saving attributes. So you must go to bed now and get rested up to receive her thanks. You're going to have a cup of hot broth and a good rest and perhaps a nap, and you'll wake up just as bright and happy as ever."

And Mrs. Rose's treatment was just what Dolly needed. She slept an hour or more and then awoke to find Dotty's black eyes gazing into her own.

"You beautiful, splendid Dollyrinda!" she exclaimed. "You're a Red Cross heroine and a Legion of Honour Girl and I don't know what all!"

"Nonsense, Dot; I didn't do any more than you did. If you hadn't had the gumption to run and get your father, Gladys would—well,—things would have been different."

"It was all my fault, though," and the tears came into Dotty's eyes. "I did the wrong in putting the baby in the canoe in the first place."

"I did that just as much as you did. We both did wrong there, I expect. And we both did wrong in scrabbling over the rope. Oh, we did wrong all right, but neither of us was worse than the other. What will Mrs. Norris say to us?"

"She's here now," said Dotty, "waiting for you to come down. She doesn't blame us, she blames Sarah for going away and leaving the baby."

"That isn't fair!" and Dolly sprang out of bed; "we told Sarah she could go. Tie up my hair, please, Dotty, I want to go down and tell Mrs. Norris all about it."

But as it turned out, Mrs. Norris was so glad and happy that little Gladys was safe, that she wouldn't allow the two D's to be blamed at all. And as the girls besought her not to blame the nurse, for what had really been their doing, they all agreed to ignore the question of blame and dwell only on their gladness and happiness at the safety of everybody concerned.

CHAPTER XII

WHO WAS THE TALL PHANTOM?

"What is a phantom party?" asked Dolly.

"Oh, it's lots of fun," Dotty replied; "everybody is rigged up in sheets, with a head-thing made of a pillow-case, and a little white mask over your face, so nobody knows you."

"Can I go?" asked Genie, her black eyes dancing.

"No," said her mother, "you're too young, dearie, this party of Edith Holmes' is an evening party; it begins at seven o'clock and only the big girls can go to it."

"Oh, dear, will I ever get grown up!" and Genie sighed with envy of her sister and Dolly.

"But how do you know who anybody is?" went on Dolly, who had never heard of this game before.

"You don't! that's the fun of it. You can't tell the girls from the boys, and you must try to make your voice different, so nobody will know who you are. Have you plenty of sheets, Mother, to fix us up?"

"Yes, indeed; one apiece will do you I think, if they are wide ones."

"We'll make our own masks," said Dotty, who had attended parties of this sort before.

So they cut masks from white muslin, with a little frill across the bottom and holes to fit their eyes.

"Now we must put a piece of gauze or net behind these eye-holes," said Dotty, out of her full experience, "for if we don't, they'd know your eyes and mine in a minute, Dollyrinda."

"Then how can we see where we're going?"

"Oh, we can see through the thin stuff easily enough, but our eyes don't show plainly to other people."

So insets of fine white net were put in the eye-holes and the dainty white masks were really pretty affairs.

They had made them not exactly alike, lest duplicates should lead to suspicion of their identity.

When it was time to get ready for the party Mrs. Rose pinned the girls into their sheet draperies.

"Make us as different as possible, Mother," advised Dotty, "so they'll never think we're us."

Mrs. Rose pinned Dolly's sheet into the semblance of a Japanese kimono, while she arranged Dotty's in full folds round the neck and let it hang in a Mother Hubbard effect.

Dolly's pillow-case headdress was bunched on either side of her head, like rosettes over her ears, and Dotty's hung in a plain flat fold down her back like an Italian girl's.

The masks were adjusted and the girls were ready to start. They wore white gloves and white shoes and looked like a pair of very lively ghosts.

Mr. Rose escorted them over to the Holmes Camp, or nearly there,—for it was the plan that each phantom must sneak in as stealthily as possible, in order to remain unknown.

So sometime before they reached their destination, Dotty ran on ahead, and with great manœuvring, managed to slip in unseen and saunter among the crowd already gathered.

Silently, among the trees, Mr. Rose led Dolly until he saw a good opportunity and then with a whispered "Scoot in there!" he indicated a chance for her to make her entrance, and he himself went back home.

It was dusk, not dark, but the light of the big camp fire made convenient shadows to screen the entrance of the guests.

It seemed a weird sight to Dolly as she somewhat timidly made her way in. Twenty or thirty white-robed figures were bowing and scraping or dancing wildly about or talking to each other in high squeaky voices and short sentences.

"Know me?" somebody said, stopping in front of Dolly.

The voice seemed a little familiar, and yet Dolly couldn't quite place it. It might be Jack Norris, or it might be one of the Holmes boys. But in a spirit of fun she nodded her head affirmatively, with great vigour, as if to declare that she knew the speaker perfectly well, but she would not speak herself.

"Who?" squeaked the high voice, hoping Dolly would speak and thus reveal her own identity.

But Dolly was too canny for this. Instead she joined together her thumb and forefinger of each hand and held them up to her eyes, making circles like eye-glass rims. Now, in sunny weather, Guy Holmes wore big glasses with shell rims, and as this described him fairly well, it was a stroke of triumph on Dolly's part. For it was Guy Holmes himself, and he doubled up with laughter at the clever identification.

But he shook his head as if Dolly were greatly mistaken in her guess, and so she didn't know whether she had been right or not.

When all had arrived, they danced in a circle round the fire, chanting wild sounds that had no meaning or rhythm but were supposed to be ghostlike wails and groans.

Then a game was played, under the direction of Mr. Holmes, by which it was endeavoured to learn who the different phantoms were.

Their host led them to what was really the drying-ground for the family laundry. A clothesline stretched on four posts formed a square, and from the clothesline depended brown paper bags of varying sizes, from large to tiny, each held by a slender string.

"One at a time," Mr. Holmes explained, "our ghostly friends will go into the square, and being blindfolded, will endeavour to hit a bag with a stick. If the attempt is successful the ghost may return unchallenged, but if he fail to hit a bag the others may guess from his gestures who it is."

The bags were not very near together, there being only three or four on each side of the clothesline square.

Mr. Holmes selected one of the phantoms and escorted it to the middle of the square, placed a stick in the outstretched hand, blindfolded the motionless figure, turned it round with a whirl and said, "Step forward, and hit where you choose, and see if you can bring down a bag."

The ghost was very evidently a boy, for two vigorous arms grasped the stick and with a couple of long strides the white figure stalked forward.

A vigorous blow ensued, but the stick came down between two of the bags and made no hit.

"Now you may guess who it is," said Mr. Holmes, "as our friend ghost did not strike anything. If you guess right, he must take off his mask, but if not he may retain it. Only one guess allowed."

Somebody sung out the name of Jack Norris, as the ghost was about his height, but the white figure shook its head vigorously and glided back among the crowd.

The game went on. Sometimes a ghost would hit a bag and the flimsy paper would burst and a quantity of peanuts or popcorn would scatter on the grass, to be scrabbled for by the rollicking phantoms.

One bag held confetti which scattered through the air in a gay shower of colour.

When it was Dolly's turn, she was determined that she would act as differently as possible from her usual manner and so fool everybody. After she was blindfolded and turned round, she took the stick and with little mincing steps, imitated exactly the gait of Josie Holmes. She made a wild dash with the stick, but failed to hit a bag and Maisie Norris called out at once, "You're Josie Holmes! I know that walk!"

Dolly shook her head vigorously and ran back to the crowd. She chanced to stand next to a very tall ghost who gravely patted her cheek as she stood beside him. Dolly looked up quickly, for she did not like this familiarity from a stranger, and she was sure the phantom was too tall to be any of the boys she knew. Of course, as the party was large, there were many of the guests whom Dolly had never met, and she resented the act of the stranger and drawing herself up with great dignity turned her back upon him.

But the tall ghost jumped around in front of her and patted her other cheek, the while he gave a cackling, rattling, ghostly chuckle.

To be sure Dolly's cheek was covered by her mask and the ghost wore white cotton gloves, but she did not at all like his familiar manner and she walked quickly away from him.

A few moments later the tall ghost himself went to take his turn with the stick.

Blindfolded and whirled about, he went with short, steady steps straight forward, and with a big whack he chanced to bring down a good sized bag. It was filled with the feathers of a whole pillow, and great laughter ensued as, like snowflakes, the feathers flew through the air. His heavy stroke had sent the bag flying upward and as it burst the feathers descended in a shower.

Since he had broken a bag, the identity of the tall ghost was not even guessed at, so Dolly had no chance to learn his name.

However, everybody was laughing and sneezing, as the feathers drifted down and flew into their mouths or tickled their ears.

Only a few of the ghosts' names were guessed correctly, as many of them had carefully disguised their shapes and sizes. Thin people had put on sweaters or bulky coats to make themselves appear stout, and short people had built up high headdresses in an effort to seem taller.

By the time the game was over every one was in most hilarious mood, and the few who had been guessed and so had removed their masks, were teasing the others in efforts to make them talk.

"I know you," said Elmer Holmes, pausing in front of Dolly. "You're Dotty Rose!"

"How do you know?" And Dolly spoke in low, guttural tones, way down in her throat.

"Oh, you needn't growl like a little bear cub! I know you, because you're so careful of that left wing of yours. You thought nobody would notice it, did you? But I spied it, and I know you're Dot! You've got on a couple of coats or something to make you look fatter, but you're Dotty, all right."

Dolly shook with laughter, for she had pretended to shield her left arm with a gesture that was purposely copied from Dotty.

Just then the tall ghost appeared again at Dolly's side. He laid his hand on her shoulder and bent down a little to look in her eyes.

Dolly drew away from him and turned to Elmer Holmes.

"Who?" she said, in a hoarse whisper, pointing to the tall phantom.

"That's telling," said Elmer, laughing. "Ask him yourself who he is."

"Who?" grunted Dolly again, addressing herself to the tall one.

"Peter, Peter, Pumpkin-Eater!" and the tall ghost grunted out the words from one corner of his mouth and Dolly could not recognise the voice. As the ghost spoke he patted Dolly on the head.

Dolly disliked his manner, for none of the other boys were other than correctly formal and polite, so she turned away from him, making a gesture of dismissal with her hand.

Apparently "Peter, Peter, Pumpkin-Eater" was desolated, for he put his hands to his eyes and rocked himself back and forth with wailing groans of despair. He was funny, and Dolly had a great desire to know who he might be, but she did not like the familiarity of his manner, and she turned away to speak to some one else.

"Take partners for a Virginia reel," called out Mr. Holmes, "and after that, we will unmask for supper."

The next moment Dolly found the tall ghost bowing before her and evidently asking her to dance with him.

But instinctively she felt that she preferred not to dance with a partner who was what she called "fresh" in his manner and she shook her head in refusal.

"Peter" urged and begged her, in dumb show, to consent. Dolly was tempted to do so, for his gestures were pleasantly wheedlesome, but as she held out her hand in half consent, Peter grasped it and falling on one knee kissed it with his hand on his heart with all the effect of a most devoted cavalier.

"He's too silly!" Dolly thought to herself; "I won't dance with him, for I don't know how he would carry on. But I wonder who he is."

So Dolly turned decidedly away from the tall suitor and found two other ghosts bowing before her and evidently requesting her to dance.

She looked at the two figures and having no idea who they might be, she hesitated which to choose.

Finally, with a white-gloved finger, she touched each in turn, "counting out."

"My—mother—told—me—to—take—this—one!" She mumbled, in a monotonous singsong tone.

And then as her final choice rested on one of the ghosts, she went away with him to take her place in the lines that were forming for the dance.

Dolly was at the end of the line of girls and opposite her, of course, was her partner. Next to Dolly's partner stood the tall ghost and as Dolly looked at him, he waved his hand at her and then lightly blew her a kiss from the tips of his white-gloved fingers.

"Freshy!" said Dolly to herself. "I think he's horrid! to act like that, when he doesn't know me at all, for I know I've not met any boy up here as tall as he is."

The dance began and there was much gay laughter as the phantoms advanced and retreated in their respective turns. The boys pranced awkwardly in their unaccustomed draperies, while the girls minced around prettily and flung their sheets in graceful whirls.

When it came Dolly's turn, she suddenly realised that as the tall ghost stood next to her own partner it was the obnoxious Peter with whom she would have to go through the figures of the old-fashioned dance.

With a very stately air she went forward as the tall ghost came to meet her half-way. They bowed with great dignity and turned to their places while the other couple did their part.

Next they must join right hands and swing around and this time the tall ghost whirled Dolly around so vigorously that he almost swung her off her feet.

Dolly began to be really annoyed, but she determined not to show it and stepped gracefully up for the next figure. This was the left hand twirl, and Peter turned her around more gently this time, but the next, when they joined both hands, Peter swung her swiftly round twice instead of once, his own feet clumping as if in a clog dance.

The next time the pair merely walked round each other back to back, and Dolly was very careful to keep as far distant as possible from the obnoxious Peter.

The dance would soon be over, she knew, and then he would have to unmask and she could see who this unpleasantly forward youth might be.

It was during the last of the grand march when it came Dolly's turn to dance gaily down the line with her own partner, whom she did not yet know by name, that Peter unceremoniously pushed Dolly's partner aside, and himself taking Dolly's hand, whirled her down the long aisle between the two lines of ghosts who clapped their hands and chanted or whistled in time to the music.

So rapidly did Peter whirl Dolly around that she had no choice but to follow, and she realised suddenly that the tall ghost was a most awkward dancer, and that unless she was very nimble herself he would tread on her toes.

Too angry now to think of disguising her voice, Dolly whispered to Peter as they danced along. "You are most rude and unmannerly! I have never met a boy so fresh and horrid! As soon as we reach the other end of the line I command you to let me go and I wish you never to speak to me again!"

Dolly was thoroughly angry, but as she preferred not to let the others know of her annoyance, she danced on with Peter toward the end of the line, though she suddenly realised that he was guiding her so as to make their progress as slow as possible.

"Oh, now,—oh, now, don't get mad!" and the squeaky voiced, choked with laughter, was almost inaudible.

"I am mad! I hate you! you're not a nice boy at all, and I wonder Edith Holmes invited you!"

"She didn't!" was squeaked into Dolly's ear, and then, as they reached the end of the line the audacious Peter lifted the frill of Dolly's mask and kissed her cheek. Then with a bow, he released her and turned away to his place in the line.

But as Peter had taken the place of Dolly's partner, and as her partner had apparently not resented this act, Dolly had no choice but to join hands with Peter and march back under an arch-way formed by the clasped hands of the other ghosts. Rather than make an unpleasant scene by refusing, Dolly thought better to do this, as it would end the dance. So giving her finger-tips to the horrid Peter she bent to go under the raised hands.

Tall Peter had to bend a great deal, and as for some reason or other he was decidedly clumsy with his feet and forever tripping on his trailing robe, the pair could think of nothing but their progress along the line, and as they reached the end, the dance was over and the music stopped.

"Now," thought Dolly to herself, "I'll see who that horrid boy is, though of course it's no one I know, and as he said Edith didn't invite him, he must be some intruder who hasn't any business here. But I can't see why he picked me out to annoy with his bad manners. I hope nobody saw him."

"Masks off!" sang out Mr. Holmes, and each ghost began to untie the strings of his concealing disguise. It was not always easy and many had to ask help from their neighbours before they could release themselves.

Dolly untied her mask quickly and stood with angry eyes awaiting a revelation of Peter's identity.

With one hand behind his head, as he loosened his mask, the tall ghost stepped to Dolly's side and said in a squeaky whisper, "Won't you forgive me?"

"No," said Dolly sternly, as she frowned at him. "You have been unpardonable, and I have no wish to know you."

"Aw, now, Dollydoodle," and the mask was whisked off and smiling down at her stood—Dolly's brother, Bert!

Dolly stared at him in utter amazement and then burst into laughter as she realised what it all meant.

"You goose!" she exclaimed, as the brother and sister stood choking with laughter at the situation.

"But how could I know you?" said Dolly, "What makes you so tall?"

"I have big blocks of wood fastened to my shoe soles," explained Bert, "and, my, but it makes me clumsy-footed!"

"I should think so! I don't see how you danced at all! Where did you come from? How did you get here? Oh, Bert, I'm so glad it was you, for I was so mad when I thought some stranger was acting up like that."

"It was a shame, Dollypops, to tease you, but I just couldn't help it. I had no intention of acting up like that, but when I just patted your hand you got so mad, that I thought it would be fun to go on. I'm glad you are such a little touch-me-not."

"Well, I should hope I wouldn't want strange boys patting me like that! And when you kissed me, Bert, I thought I should scream, I was so mad, but honestly I was ashamed to make a scene and let people know what you had done."

"You'll forgive me, sister, won't you?" and Bert's big blue eyes looked into Dolly's, as for a moment he did feel ashamed of himself for teasing her so. But his love of a joke was so great, that he had thoroughly enjoyed fooling Dolly and his affectionate sister willingly forgave him.

"Don't know yet who was your partner, do you, Dolly?" said a voice near her, and turning, Dolly saw Bob Rose.

"Oh, were you?" and Dolly turned to him, laughing.

"I sure was! I resigned in favour of Bert at the last, because he commanded me to."

"When did you come up here?" and the amazed Dolly began to realise how matters stood.

"To-night," said Bert. 'We were at Crosstrees before you girls left, but Mrs. Rose kept us hidden and after you were gone, she togged us up in sheets, and here we are."

"But why did you make yourself tall, Bert? Nobody up here would know you anyhow, except Dot and me."

"Oh, just did it for fun. Thought I'd make an impression as the tallest ghost in captivity. Where's Dotty? And I want to meet a few of these other ghost girls. I'll shake you now, Dollikins, and you can have your own partner back." Bert went away leaving Bob with Dolly, who escorted her to supper.

The supper was served in true camp-fire fashion. There was no table, the ghosts, all unmasked now, sat round the big fire on camp stools or cushions, and the boys waited on the girls in true picnic style. There were substantial viands, as the evening air caused hearty appetites, and Dolly settled herself comfortably on a divan improvised of evergreen boughs and gratefully accepted a cup of hot bouillon and some sandwiches that Bob brought.

Edith Holmes was sitting by Dolly, and she was chuckling with laughter as Bert told her the joke he had played on his sister.

After supper the merry young people sang songs and glees round the fire until it was time to go home.

"Daddy said he'd come for us," said Dotty laughingly to Dolly, "but of course he didn't mean it for he knew the boys would be here to take us home."

"I'll just remove these blocks of wood before I start," said Bert, as he quickly tore off the clumsy and cumbersome things.

"Now I can walk better," and he stood on his own shoe soles and at his own height.

"I'm awfully glad you're here again, Bob," said Edith Holmes, as they said good-night, "and I'm glad you're here too," she added to Bert Fayre. "Our camps are so near that we must play together a lot."

"Nice girl," commented Bert, as the quartette walked away. "Lots of nice people at that party."

"Yes," agreed Bob, "girls are nice at parties, but sometimes we don't want them around. Be sure to be up, old man, by sunrise tomorrow morning, for we're going fishing early."

"Can't we go?" asked Dotty.

"No, ma'am! No girls need apply. A real fishing trip is a serious matter and we can't be bothered with girls. When we come home tomorrow night, if Mother says you've been good children all day, you can have some of our fish."

CHAPTER XIII

THAT LUNCHEON

To Dolly's surprise she discovered that Bob and Bert were in earnest regarding their preference for expeditions that did not include girls. Nearly every day the two boys went off fishing or motor boating with a lot of their cronies, but the girls were seldom asked.

"They're always like that," said Dotty, carelessly. "They like to ramble through the woods or cruise around the lake by themselves. They wear old flannel shirts and disreputable hats, and they eat their lunch any old way, without any frills or fuss. I don't like that sort of picnicking myself, I like pretty table fixings even if they're only paper napkins and pasteboard dishes. But the boys like tin pails and old frying pans and they catch their fish and cook 'em and eat 'em like a horde of savages."

"All right," agreed Dolly, "we can have fun enough without them; but I think they might take us along sometimes. Let's get up a rival picnic some day, and see if they won't come to it."

"They won't," said Dotty, "but we can try it, if you like. And anyway we can have our own fun."

So one day when all the boys of the neighbouring camps were going on a fishing trip, the girls arranged a picnic of their own.

The two Holmes girls, Maisie Norris, Dolly and Dotty, and three or four others, were in the crowd and they were to go in two motor boats to Bramble Brook, the very spot where the boys were trout fishing that day.

Long Sam navigated one boat and the Norris's man engineered the other.

Dolly had evolved a plan for a great joke on the boys, which, she flattered herself, would even up with Bert for the joke he had played on her.

In pursuance of their plan, the girls were taking with them a most marvellous luncheon.

There were boxes of devilled eggs, each gold and white confection in a case of fringed white paper. Sandwiches in tiny rolls and fancy shapes. Dishes of salad that were pictures in themselves, and platters of cold meats cut in appetising slices and garnished with aspic jelly in quivering translucence. Platters of cold chicken, delicately browned and garnished with parsley and lemon slices.

Dainty baskets of little frosted cakes and tartlets filled with tempting jam covered with frosting.

Oh, Dolly had planned well for her little joke, and if successful, it would be rare sport.

The boys had been gone for hours when the girls started, and in their fresh linen dresses and bright hair-ribbons they were a jolly looking crowd who filled the two motor boats as they left the Crosstrees pier.

Mrs. Rose waved a good-bye, knowing the young people were safe, in charge of Long Sam and old Ephraim, the tried and trusted factotum of the Norris family.

"In you go!" cried Long Sam as he deftly handed the girls into the boats, and the laughing crowd settled themselves to enjoy the trip.

It was a beautiful mid-summer day, and the heat sufficiently tempered by the cool breezes that swept across the lake. The girls chattered and sang and called to each other as the two boats kept close together on their way.

When they reached Bramble Brook they did not go to the regular landing place, but Long Sam cleverly found a concealed nook where they could land without danger of being seen by the boys who were already there.

The trout stream was a long one, but all of its meanderings were well known to Sam and Ephraim, who were old residents of the locality.

The girls waited while the two men went to reconnoitre.

After a time the scouts returned.

"They're away up the brook," said Long Sam, "but all their grub and things is stacked in the clearing, and I reckon they'll be coming along back in about an hour to feed. They started pretty early and I reckon they can't hold out much longer 'thout their grub. What next, ladies?"

"You, Sam, help us unpack our hampers," said Dolly, who was directing affairs, "and you, Ephraim, go and gather up all their foodstuff and either hide it around there or bring it back here."

"Yes'm," and old Ephraim trudged away, intent only on obeying orders to the letter.

He returned with a big basket on either arm.

"Thought I'd better fetch it along," he said; "them chaps would hunt it out wherever I hid it. I left 'em all their cooking things, pots and pans, but poor fellers, they won't have nothin' to cook!"

"Here's their coffee," cried Edith Holmes, who was peering into the baskets. "And here's bacon and eggs, oh, what horrid looking stuff! And loaves of dry bread! Guy and Elmer just hate plain bread. May be they won't care for our sandwiches!"

"Let's make coffee!" said Dotty; "there's nothing so good at a camp feast as coffee. Don't you love it, Edith?"

"Mother doesn't let me have it, but make it all the same, the boys adore it."

"We can have one cup," said Dotty; "Mother allows that. But I'm going to make it, the boys will be crazy about it. You scoot back and get the coffee pot, Ephraim, and the big long spoon, they'll probably have one."

Back went Ephraim on his errand, and when he returned his eyes were greeted by the sight of the daintily spread luncheon.

Heavy brown papers had been spread on the ground, and these were covered with a tablecloth of white crepe paper with a design of green ferns for a border. Real ferns were laid here and there under the dishes of good things, and piles of white pasteboard plates and paper napkins were in readiness.

"What about coffee cups?" exclaimed Maisie. "I know they only have horrid old tin things."

"Oh, we've lots of paper drinking cups," said Dotty, "those pretty pleated ones, they'll be lovely for coffee. Say, Sam, I want this coffee to be just right, and I wish you'd make it. I know how, but I'm sure yours will be better."

Long Sam was greatly flattered at this compliment, and he proceeded to build a fire and make the coffee with a practised hand that betokened long experience in these arts.

"Isn't the table lovely!" exclaimed Josie Holmes, as she brought a few wild flowers she had found, and placed them gracefully among the ferns that decorated the feast.

"And thank goodness I haven't seen a spider nor an ant!" cried Nellie North, who had been, with another girl, told off to keep the table free of any such marauders. One venturesome grasshopper had made a spring toward the food, but had been caught and had his energies turned in a far different direction.

"S'pose we have to wait an awful long time," said Edith, as she looked longingly at the tempting dishes.

"Never mind if we do!" said Dotty; "there's nothing that can take any hurt. There's nothing to get cold except the coffee, and Sam will attend to that. The glass fruit jars full of lemonade are in the brook, so that will be lovely and cool when we want it. Oh, everything is all right; and we've only just got to wait. So you girls may as well make up your mind to it."

Although the wait seemed long, after a time, Long Sam,

scouting about, heard the boys' voices in the distance. He warned the girls and they were all quiet as mice, awaiting developments.

The crowd of boys came nearer, laughing and shouting, as they reached their own headquarters.

Sam beckoned to the girls to come and peep through the bushes at the amazed group, who had suddenly discovered that their food was missing.

"Somebody has swiped it!" cried Elmer Holmes, angrily. "All our grub is gone! I say, fellows, what shall we do?"

"Do! Go after them and get it back!" cried Jack Norris, and then a chorus of shouts went up; "the coffee pot's gone!" "All the bacon and eggs are gone!" "And the bread, too!"

"They sure made a clean sweep," said Bert Fayre. "Who do you s'pose did it?"

"Some other crowd of fishing chaps," said Bob Rose, confidently, "but it doesn't often happen,—a thing like that. No decent fellows would do it."

The girls, only a few rods distant, were peeping through the bushes and shaking with silent laughter at the discomfited boys. Such looks of chagrin and dismay as they showed! and such belligerent determination to hunt the marauders and duly punish them.

"Just you wait till I get hold of the thieves!" cried Elmer Holmes, "I'll give them what for!"

"You won't catch them," said Bert; "they're probably miles away by this time, and they've probably eaten up all our snacks. Wow, but I'm hungry!"

"So say we all of us!" chorused the boys, as they flung themselves around in disconsolate attitudes.

"Not a snip-jack of anything," Jack went on, peering vainly into a few empty baskets that Sam had left behind him. "The nerve of them, to steal our coffee and then take our coffee pot to make it in! Honest, fellows, I never knew such a thing to happen before. I've been up here a lot of summers and I never struck a crowd that would do such a thing as this."

"That's so," agreed Bob Rose, "why, often a lot of strange chaps will share their grub with you, but I never knew 'em to hook it! Must be an awful mean crowd."

"Well, all the same," said Bert, "what are we going to do for lunch? I rousted out at sunup, and to be sure, I had my breakfast, but it's forgotten in the dim past."

"We can cook our fish," said one of the boys "but we'll miss the coffee and potatoes and bread and such various staffs of life. We haven't such a lot of fish anyhow."

"No; we depended on bacon and eggs for our mainstay. I move we go home."

"S'pose we'll have to," and Bob looked rueful, "We can't put in a whole afternoon on empty stomachs. What do you say, shall we cook the fish, or light right out for home?"

"Here's a cracker they dropped," cried Bert, who spied a soda biscuit on the ground and brushing it off, began to eat it.

"Aw, give a starving comrade a bite," and Guy held out his hand eagerly.

"By jiminy, here's another!" and Jack found another cracker farther along.

Now this was part of the plan, and it was at Dolly's directions that Long Sam had carefully planted a few crackers at intervals to lure the unsuspecting boys to the surprise that awaited them.

Dolly and Dotty, with their arms around each other, were peeping through the trees, and they shook with glee as they saw the boys eagerly hunting for the stray crackers.

"Funny how they came to drop 'em along," said Guy and Elmer responded, "Must have been eating them on their way. But say, they've left a trail; let's follow it."

The group of boys—there were eight of them—moved slowly along toward where the girls were hidden. The trail of crackers had been adroitly arranged to bring them finally within sight of the appetising luncheon so daintily set forth.

As the boys came nearer to the little clearing, and as the sight of the feast must in a moment burst upon their eyes, the girls scampered to hide behind trees to watch the astonished faces.

Nor were they disappointed. In a moment more the boys came in sight of the luncheon and stopped suddenly.

"By gum!"

"Well, what do you know about that!"

"Jiminy crickets!"

"Ah there, my size!"

And various other boyish exclamations gave voice to surprise and delight on the part of the onlookers. But they paused several steps away from the feast.

"That's a girls' layout," said Bert Fayre, nodding his head sagaciously; "no fellows ever set up that dinky business! But it looks good to me!"

"Good!" exclaimed Jack; "I'd face a term in State's prison to nab that loot! Wonder who owns it!"

"Certainly not the people who stole our grub; so we can't claim this in return. Oh, I smell coffee! 'M-mm!"

Unwilling to intrude further on what was so evidently a girls' picnic, and yet equally unable to tear themselves away from the enticing scene, the boys stood, a comically eager crowd, looking vainly about for signs of the picnic party.

"Seems 'sif I must grab one sandwich," said Bob, rolling his eyes comically toward the piled-up dishes.

"Well, you won't," said Bert, who had no fear that Bob would be guilty of such a thing, but he wasn't quite so sure of some of the other boys, and so they stood like a lot of hungry tramps, a little bewildered at the situation and greatly tantalised by the sight of the feast and the odour of steaming coffee.

"Nothing doing," said Bob, at last. "We can't touch other people's property, and we might as well go on home. But if the ladies belonging to this church sociable would show themselves, I'd sit up and beg for a bone of that fried chicken over there."

"Maybe we all wouldn't!" commented several, and then, at a signal from Dolly, the girls sprang from their hiding-places and stood laughing at the crowd of hungry boys.

"Oh, you Dotty Rose!" cried Jack Norris, as he caught Dotty's dancing black eyes, "I might have known you were at the head of this!"

"No more than Dolly Fayre," cried Dotty, "and all the rest of us. Are you hungry, boys?"

"Are we hungry? We should smile! We've been hungry all the while!" came in chorus from the famished tramps.

"Would you care to come to lunch with us?" said Dolly, her blue eyes dancing as she put the question.

"Would we care to!" and Jack grinned at her. "We're hungry enough to eat you girls; but, alas! kind ladies, we're obliged to regret your invitation as we're not in proper society garb."

Suddenly the boys became aware of their flannel shirts and old hats and general fishermanlike appearance.

"We'll forgive that for once," cried Dotty; "we'll pretend we're a rescue party and you're a lot of starving soldiers, so we won't mind your tattered uniforms."

"Rescue party!" cried Bob; "I like that! Aren't you the sly ones who raided our commissariat department? Own up, now!"

"What makes you think so?" And Edith Holmes looked the picture of injured innocence.

"Oh, yes! 'What makes us think so!' What makes us think that's our coffee boiling in our coffee pot! Fair ladies, we invite you to lunch with us, on our coffee and our bacon and eggs. And if you'll wait a few minutes, we'll cook our trout for you."

"Well, I'll tell you what," and golden-haired Dolly settled the question; "we'll eat our luncheon now, as it's all ready, and then, if you like, you can cook your fish afterward."

"That suits me," said Bob, "and I'm free to confess that I can't wait another minute to attack this Ladies'-Own-Cooking-School Lay Out! Take seats, everybody— I mean you girls sit down, and us chaps will wait on you."

"All right," laughed Dolly; "we resign in your favour. I can tell you girls get hungry, too."

So the girls sat around, and the boys quickly passed plates and napkins and then the dishes of delicious food.

Then they served themselves, and sitting down by the girls, rapidly demolished the contents of their well-filled plates.

"I'm not going to rub it in," said Dolly, dimpling with smiles, "but for boys who don't want girls along on their picnics you seem to enjoy our society fairly well."

"It isn't our society they're enjoying," said Nellie North; "it's our stuffed eggs and cold chicken."

"It's both, adorable damsels," declared Bob. "Just let us appease our hunger, and goodness knows you've enough stuff here for a regiment, and then we'll show you how we appreciate the blessing of your society. We'll entertain you any way you choose."

"That we will," agreed Guy. "We'll give you a circus performance, a concert, lecture, or song and dance, as you decree."

But it took a long time to satisfy the boys' appetites. It seemed as if they could never get enough of the various delicacies, and though they pretended to make fun of what they called the fiddly-faddly frills, they thoroughly relished the good things.

"These eggs ought to be shaved," said Bob, as he picked the little fringes of white tissue paper from a devilled egg.

"No critical remarks, please," said Dolly, offering him a rolled up sandwich tied with a narrow white ribbon.

"Oh, my goodness! do I eat ribbon and all? I can do magical stunts for you afterward, like the chap who pulls yards of ribbon out of his mouth, on the stage."

"Anybody who makes fun of our things can't have any," declared Josie.

"Oh, I'm not making fun," and Bob took half a dozen of the tiny sandwiches. "Why, I always have my meals tied up in ribbons. I have sashes on my griddle-cakes and neckties on my eggs, always."

"I like these orange-peel baskets filled with fruit salad," said Bert, as he helped himself to another; "I think food in baskets is the only real proper way."

But at last, even the hungry fishermen declared they couldn't eat another bite, and the young people left the feast and sat on the rocks and tree stumps near by, while Long Sam and Ephraim cleared away and packed up the things to take home.

The boys were as good as their word, and entertained the girls by singing college songs and giving gay imitations and stunts, and everybody declared, as the picnic finally broke up, that it had been the very best one of the season.

CHAPTER XIV

THE CAKE CONTEST

"Oh, do go in for it!" Edith Holmes was saying, as she and Maisie Norris sat on the edge of the Rose's shack and tried to persuade Dotty and Dolly to agree to their plan.

"But I never made a cake in my life," Dolly objected.

"Nor I, either," said Dotty; "I don't see how we can, Edith. You're a regular born cook, and that's different."

"But maybe you're a regular born cook, too," argued Edith; "you can't tell if you never have tried."

"Anyway, enter the contest just for fun," urged Maisie. "Everybody will help with the bazaar, and of course you want to be in it; and I want you to be in this contest, because all us girls are."

"I'd just as lieve," said Dolly, "only there's no chance of our winning the prize."

"Well, never mind if you don't. You'll have a lot of fun, and besides it will teach you to make cake, and that's a good thing to know. That funny old Maria of yours will help you."

"But would it be fair to have her help us?"

"Oh, of course not make the cake; you must do that yourselves. But she can tell you how, or show you how, and you can practise all you like beforehand, of course. And you might win the prize, after all."

"What is the prize?"

"A twenty dollar gold piece!"

"What a grand prize! I didn't know it was such a big one."

"Well, you see, old Mrs. Van Zandt gives it. She's a crank on Domestic Science and girls knowing how to cook and all that. And besides there'll be lots of entries. All the girls all round the lake will send cakes."

"Can anybody send?"

"Any girl under sixteen. They call it the Sweet Sixteen Cake Prize."

"All right, let's do it," said Dotty, and Dolly said, "I'm willing, but it seems nonsensical when we don't know a thing about making cake, and less than a week to learn in. But we can have a try at it, anyway, and we'll be in the fun. Hey, Dotsy?"

"All right, then," said Maisie, delightedly; "I'll tell Miss Travers that you two girls will join the contest. She'll be delighted. She's at the head of that committee."

99

Later the two D's conferred with Mrs. Rose about the matter.

"I'll be glad to have you do it," that lady said. "I always like to have you learn anything domestic. Of course you can learn to make cake in a week, if you have any knack at all. Go down to the kitchen now, and Maria will give you your first lessons. Ask her to show you how to make plain cup-cake first, and if you make a little more elaborate kind every day, by the end of the week you ought to be able to concoct almost anything. I don't want to be discouraging, but I can hardly think you'll take the prize, for I remember last year the cakes were really most astonishing affairs."

"No, we won't catch any prize," Dotty agreed; "but we want to be in the bazaar, and the cake department is about as much fun as any. You see, even if we don't take the prize, we sell our cakes for the biggest price possible and that helps the bazaar along."

"Is it for charity?" asked Dolly.

"Yes; they hold it every year in the hotel, and all the camp people take part. Oh, it's lots of fun; I'm so glad it's going to be while you're here."

The two girls ran down to the kitchen, and informed Maria of their immediate desire to learn to make cake.

"Bress gracious, chillun," said the surprised old coloured woman, "I'll make all de cakes you all can eat. Don't you bodder 'bout makin' cakes yo'self. Jes' leab dat to ole Maria."

"But you don't understand, Cookie," said Dotty. "We want to learn, because we're going to make a cake to send to the fair, for the prize contest."

"Prize contes'! What's dat?"

"Why, they give a prize for the best cake sent in."

"All right, den. Leab it all to me. I'll sho'ly make a cake what'll catch dat prize. You all shoo out ob here now."

"No, no, Maria, you don't understand," and Dolly began to explain. "We must make the cakes ourselves. You can't do it, because you're not under sixteen—are you?" And the laughing blue eyes looked quizzically at the old darky.

"Sixteen! Laws, chile, I's a mudder in Israel. I got chilluns and grandchilluns. I ain't been sixteen since I can 'member. But, lawsy,—a young un of sixteen can't make no cake worth eatin'!"

"But we can, if you teach us, Maria," said Dotty, with tactful flattery.

"Well, mebbe dat's so, if I do the most of it, and you jes' bring me the things."

"No, that won't do; we must do it ourselves, but you must show us how."

At last they convinced Maria of her part in the undertaking, and

100

with more or less good-natured grumbling, she proceeded to enlighten the girls in the mysteries of cake making.

The old cook was not trammelled by definite recipes and her rules seemed to be "a little of dis," and "a right smart lot of dat."

But, even so, she was a good teacher, and at the end of the first lesson, the girls had each a round cake, plain, but light and wholesome, well-baked and delicately browned.

These were proudly exhibited at the family luncheon, and were at once appropriated by Bob and Bert, who immediately constituted themselves a Court of Final Judgment, and declared their intention of eating all the preliminary cakes that would be made during the week's lessons.

So interested did the girls become, that every morning they spent in the kitchen.

Mr. Rose expressed a mock terror lest his bills for butter and eggs should land him in the poor-house, but the cake-making went on, and more and more elaborate confections were turned out by the rapidly progressing cooks.

Mrs. Rose declared that it was her opinion that doctors' bills were imminent, if indeed the whole family would not soon be in the hospital; but though the boys and Genie ate a fair portion of the cakes, much more was consumed by the neighbouring young people, who formed a habit of drifting in to Crosstrees camp afternoons to sample the morning's work.

The days brought plum cakes and marble cakes; chocolate, cocoanut, custard and jelly cakes.

Once having achieved the knack of making the cake itself, the fillings or elaborations were not difficult.

The girls took the matter rather seriously, but as the great day drew nearer, they began to have a glimmering hope that they might achieve the prize after all.

"But, oh, Dollyrinda," exclaimed Dotty, impulsively, "if my cake should take the prize ahead of yours, I'd cry my eyes out, and if your cake took the prize ahead of mine, I'd never speak to you again!"

Dolly laughed. "I've been thinking about that, too, Dot, and do you know, I think it would be nicest for us to make only one cake, and make it together, and enter it under both our names, and then if it takes the prize we can divide the twenty dollars."

Dotty drew a long sigh of relief. "That is the best way, Doll; I never thought of that. To be sure we run a double chance with two cakes, but it would be horrid for one of them to take the prize. So let's devote all our energies to one beautiful, splendiferous cake that will be so perfect nobody else will have any chance at all."

"Yes, that's what I think. Now, what kind shall it be?"

This was the great question. The girls had proved apt pupils, for they had a housewifely knack, and Maria was really a superior teacher. They had learned the art of pound cake, the trick of sponge cake and had even penetrated the mysteries of fruit cake. They had learned to make raisin cake without having all the raisins sink to a thick mat at the bottom; they had learned ginger-bread in all its forms, from the puffy golden sort to the most dark spicy variety. Angel food and sunshine cake presented no difficulties to them and layer cakes were their happy hunting ground.

Also they were Past Grand Masters in the matter of icing. They could boil sugar through its seven stages of spun thread, and they even experimented with a few confectioners' implements in the matter of fancy decoration and borders.

"It seems to me," said Dotty, as they held solemn conclave over the great question, "that our trick is to invent an absolutely new combination of flavours or ingredients. Say, cocoanut stirred into chocolate icing, or something that's different from the regulation 'White mountain cake' or 'Variety cake.' I'm sure we can think of some new idea that will be perfectly stunning."

"I don't agree with you, Dot," and Dolly looked solemnly thoughtful, as her blue eyes stared into Dotty's black ones. "Now, I think this way. A more simple cake, but of perfect quality and with a plain but beautiful icing, that will charm by its very simplicity."

"That's a fine line of talk, Doll, and sounds well," put in Bert, who was present with Bob as Advisory Board; "but I doubt if 'twill go down with the Powers that Be. You see, after all, they're on the lookout for novelty and elaborate messes."

"I'm not so sure of that," and Bob shook his head. "Perhaps Dolliwop's idea isn't so worse! It's like a beautiful big white monument being more impressive than a lot of ginger-bread architecture."

"Oh, we wouldn't make ginger-bread!" cried Dotty, laughing; "but I can't see a plain cake taking a prize. I tell you, it's got to have an unusual combination of materials. I can't get away from the idea that a novel mixture of just the right kind of flavouring would turn the trick."

"And I'm positive that simplicity is the note to strike for." Dolly said this with a faraway look in her eyes, as if she saw the vision of the beautiful cake she was planning.

"Stick to it, Doll," cried Bob. "You've got the right idea or I'm a loser!"

"You boys go away, now," and Dolly's brows wrinkled in serious thought. "This is no time for fooling and Dot and I have to decide this thing to-day."

Realising the gravity of the occasion, the boys went off, and the two girls settled down to a desperate confab. Neither of them was insistent merely because she wanted her own way, but each was eager for success, and quite ready to settle their controversy by careful weighing of each other's arguments.

At last, after a long discussion, they reached their conclusions and went down to the kitchen to construct what they had finally decided would be the best plan for their masterpiece.

Very carefully they worked, Dolly, slow, sure and very particular as to measurements and combinations; Dotty, quick, beating the batter like mad, whisking eggs and sifting sugar in a whirl of excitement.

And when the great work was accomplished, and the marvellous result set on the dining-room table for exhibition, the family came in to gaze in an awed silence on the beautiful cake.

No one was allowed to see it but the household, for of course it was kept secret from the other contestants.

The cake was a marvel of beauty, and it combined the best ideas of the plans of the two girls.

It was square in shape, instead of round, as that gave a touch of novelty. It was only two layers, but the layers were of the most exquisitely textured angel food, which had, after three attempts, graciously consented to turn out "just right."

Between the layers was a filling, which followed in a measure Dotty's idea of novelty. It was a combination of confectioners' icing, whipped cream, pineapple juice and a few delicate feathery flakes of freshly grated cocoanut. This delectable mixture was novel and of charming delicacy.

But the icing was Dolly's triumph. The square cake, large and high, was covered so smoothly with white icing that not a lump or a crack marred the perfect surface of its top and sides. There were no decorations save three lines of icing that delicately outlined the square top. The trueness of these lines was a wonder, and only Dolly's steady hand as she traced them with a paper cornucopia of icing could have resulted in such an effective scheme.

"It is perfectly wonderful!" said Mr. Rose, looking at it as an artist. "It's like the Taj Mahal or some such World Wonder."

"It's perfectly exquisite!" said Mrs. Rose, as she bent over to examine it and then walked away to view it from a distance. "I never saw such icing! How did you do it, girlies?"

"Dolly did that," said Dotty.

"Only because you were so excited your hand wiggled," said Dolly, who was always placid, whatever happened. "But the filling is

Dot's invention, and it's just fine. We put some of it on another cake and I want you all to taste it."

So they all sampled the other cake, and tested the flavour like connoisseurs.

"Ripping!" exclaimed Bob.

"Out of sight!" remarked Bert, suiting the action to the word.

The boys were vociferous, the older people were enthusiastic; but one and all agreed that there had never been such a cake built before and that it would surely win the prize.

"Are you going to send it over now?" asked Mr. Rose.

"No," said Dotty; "we're going to take it with us when we go ourselves. I wouldn't trust it to anybody, for it might get joggled and crack the icing. Put it in the pantry, Dolly; I daren't touch it myself." Dotty was quivering with excitement, but Dolly's steady hand carefully lifted the precious cake and carried it safely to the pantry.

Later in the afternoon, the girls made ready to go to the bazaar. They were to serve as assistants in the cake department, for the majority of the cakes were to be sold. The prize cake, and those having honourable mention would be exhibited, and later sold at auction, but much cake would be disposed of at the regular sale.

They wore white dresses, with pale green ribbons, which was the costume of all connected with that department of the bazaar.

Very pretty they looked, as they came dancing downstairs for Mrs. Rose's inspection.

"You'll do, girlies," she commented; "your frocks are all right. We'll be over later. I hate to have you carry that big cake, Dolly."

"Oh, I must, Mrs. Rose; I wouldn't trust it to any one else. Bert offered to take it, and Bob did, too. But if they should drop it or anything, I'd never get over the disappointment. We worked so hard on it, and it is so lovely, and if we can just get it there safely, I'm sure it will get honourable mention at least."

"It ought to take the prize," said Mrs. Rose, enthusiastically; "but don't get your hopes up too high, for there's nothing surer than disappointment. Be very careful as you get in the boat, Dolly."

"Indeed, yes, but Long Sam is such a kind old thing, I know he'll do all he can not to joggle, but to run very steadily all the way."

The bazaar was held in a hotel which was some distance down the lake. But Dolly did not fear any accident while on the motor boat; she was only apprehensive lest some one push against her as she made her way into the building or into the cake booth. For one little crumb of broken icing or one dent on its perfect surface would spoil, to Dolly's anxious eye, the perfection of their cake.

CHAPTER XV

WHO WON THE PRIZE?

"We'd better take our sweaters," said Dolly, as she handed the two white, fleecy garments to Dotty. "You carry them, Dot, and I'll carry the cake; you'd be sure to drop it."

Dotty took the two sweaters and flung them over her arm, well knowing the precious cake would be safer in Dolly's steady hand.

"Now we're all ready," Dolly said, as she tucked a handkerchief into her sash folds. "Wait for me here, Dot, and I'll get the cake."

Dolly went to the kitchen and on through to the pantry, where she had left the cake on a shelf by the window. But it was not there.

"Maria," she called, wondering what the old darky had done with it.

There was no reply and Dolly called again louder.

"Yas'm, I'se comin'," and the old cook came in at the back door of the kitchen. "What yo' want, honey? I spec' I jes' done drapped asleep fer a minute, settin' out dere in de sun. What is it, honey chile?"

"Where's the cake, Maria?"

"On de pantry shelf, whar yo' done left it. I ain't teched it, dat I ain't."

"But it isn't there. You must have put it someplace else."

"No, Miss Dolly, I nebber laid a hand on dat cake. I know jes' how choice you was of it, an' I lef it jes' whar yo' put it."

"But it isn't there, and who would disturb it?"

"Tain't dar! Land o' goodness! Den whar is it?" Maria's black eyes rolled in dismay. "Somebody's done stole it!"

"Stole it? Nonsense! Nobody would do that. Dot—ty!" and Dolly's loud call brought Dotty flying.

Mrs. Rose followed, and both stood aghast with consternation when Dolly announced, "The cake is gone!"

"Gone! What do you mean?" and Dotty looked around the shelves in a dazed sort of way.

"I mean what I say," cried Dolly impatiently. "Our cake is gone, and, as Maria says, somebody must have stolen it."

"Stolen it! Our cake!" and Dotty gave a wild shriek.

"It can't be stolen," said Mrs. Rose, looking puzzled; "we've never had anything stolen all the years we've been here."

"Then where is it?" demanded Dolly. "Where can it be?"

"Didn't you take it into the dining-room?" suggested Mrs. Rose, unable to think of any other solution of the mystery.

"No, indeed; I left it right here till we were ready to start. I had it in the open window, because the kitchen was so hot, and of course some tramp has come along and stolen it. Oh, Dotty, what shall we do?"

But Dotty was beyond speech. Her staring eyes gazed at the table where the cake had been. Vaguely she glanced round the pantry shelves, and then flew through the kitchen to the dining-room and looked all around there. But of course she saw no cake, for Dolly had left it in the pantry.

"Where are the boys?" asked Dolly, suddenly.

"Gone to a motor boat race," said Mrs. Rose. "They went off half an hour ago. But they wouldn't steal your cake."

"They might do it for a joke," said Dolly.

"No," said Mrs. Rose, decidedly; "they wouldn't do that. They were too interested in the success of you girls, and they felt about that cake just as we all did. No, Bob and Bert never stole the cake! Where's Genie?"

"Upstairs, I think," said Dotty, and going to the foot of the staircase she called her sister.

Genie came running down and was as greatly disturbed as the other girls at the disappearance of the cake.

"Of course I never touched it!" she said indignantly. "I wanted my Dotty and my Dolly to take the prize. Do you s'pose I'd steal their lovely cake?"

There was no mistaking the little girl's honesty and good faith, and Mrs. Rose said finally: "Then it must have been stolen by some one passing by, but I can't understand it. There are no tramps around here, Long Sam is as honest as the day, and nobody else would be passing by this window. I wish your father were here, Dotty."

"So do I, but he couldn't do anything. The cake's gone, and it must have been taken by somebody. What do you say if we make another, Dolly?"

Dolly looked blank. "Make another!" she said slowly; "why it's three o'clock now, and the fair begins at four. We couldn't do it, Dot, and anyway we couldn't make a prize one. I wouldn't have the heart to try again as hard as I did for that one. Would you?"

"Yes, I would! I'd just like to fly at it and make one as good as that or better! I know who stole that cake, Dorinda Fayre! It was some girl who had made a cake herself and who was afraid ours would take the prize, and so she came and stole it!"

"Oh, Dorothy Rose! aren't you ashamed to think such a thing!

And anyway, how could any girl do that even if she was mean enough?"

"Of course she could!" and Dotty's eyes flashed; "everybody knew about our cake, and they knew it would take the prize, and so of course they wanted it out of the way! Now that's just what happened, because it's the only thing that can have happened. As Mother says, there aren't any tramps around here. We always set cakes or pies on that window shelf and they've never been stolen. Come on, I say, let's make another; I hate to have any girl get ahead of me like that!"

"Oh, Dotty, it just seems as if I couldn't make another. Why we were three hours on that one this morning. It would be after six o'clock before we could get another done. And I know it wouldn't be any good, I'm too upset to make it properly. I'm all of a quiver. And besides we haven't all the things in the house."

"No, we've no pineapple. But let's make some other kind of a cake, chocolate, or something."

"Yes! I think I see a chocolate cake taking the prize! Why don't you make ginger-bread and be done with it? That prize won't go to any common kind of cake, like chocolate."

"It might if it was awful good chocolate. Oh, Dolly, our cake was so beautiful!" And Dotty's overwrought nerves gave way and she burst into violent sobbing.

"Well, crying won't do any good, Dot," and Dolly drew a long sigh; "I don't blame you for crying, 'cause I know you can't help it. But I can't seem to cry, I'm too—too flattened out."

Dolly looked the picture of disheartened woe, but it was not her nature to give way to tears. She felt absolutely dismayed and utterly cast down, as if under a depression that would not lift, but she gave no physical sign of this except by her tense, drawn face and her frequent despairing sighs.

"It's just awful, girlies," said Mrs. Rose, full of helpless sympathy; "but I can't think of anything to do. I don't believe you could make another cake successfully, you're too nervous and upset, both of you."

Maria, however, did not take it so calmly. Her grief was more boisterous even than Dolly's. She ran round the kitchen, throwing her apron over her head, and wailing and moaning like a crazy woman.

"Oh, dat cake! dat cake!" she groaned, dropping into a chair and rocking back and forth in ecstasies of woe. "Dat hebenly cake! Sho'ly Miss Dotty and Miss Dolly yo' could make anudder. I kin help yo', and we'll whisk it up in a jiffy. Do make some kind, oh do, now!"

"No, Maria," and Dolly looked positive; "we can't make another cake. It's out of the question. Shall we go to the fair at all, Dot?"

"Yes, of course we will! I want to find out what girl was mean enough and smart enough to cut up this trick!"

"Come on then. You'd better wash your face, you're all teary looking. I s'pose we might as well go, but I don't feel a bit like it. All the fun's gone out of it."

Dotty ran away to bathe her reddened eyes, and Dolly gravely walked round the kitchen, looking here and there as if the cake might have voluntarily hidden itself somewhere.

"It's most mysterious," said Mrs. Rose. "I never heard of anything being stolen up in this region before. I wish Mr. Rose were here, but of course he couldn't do anything, and I think we may feel sure that he didn't steal the cake."

"Where is he?" asked Dolly, smiling a little at the jest.

"Gone over to the Norris camp, I think. I wish the boys were here; of course they couldn't do anything, but they could help us express our indignation."

"Yes, they could do that, but it wouldn't do any real good. Hello, Dot, ready?"

The two girls started off down the path and Mrs. Rose watched them go with a sad heart. She knew how disappointed they were, after all their trouble to make the cake, and she couldn't imagine what had become of it.

"I can't believe any of the girls came and took it," she said to Maria.

"No, ma'am, dat dey didn't! dat cake was sperrited away by ghos'es. Dat's what it was!" And the big black eyes rolled in terrified apprehension. "Yas'm, sho'ly fer certain, dat's what happened. It's de work of dem sperrits!"

Mrs. Rose went on into the house unwilling to subscribe to Maria's theory, but equally unable to propound any of her own.

The girls reached the hotel where the fair was held and joined the gay throngs of people that were entering.

"Hello," said Maisie Norris as she met them. "Where's your cake?"

Now Dolly and Dotty had made up their minds not to tell of the catastrophe, until they could make some endeavour to find out if there were any suspicious looks or hints to be noticed among the other young cake makers.

"Where's yours?" Dotty said to Maisie.

"Oh, I left mine in the committee room. You know the committee take all the cakes, and then those that haven't any chance at all, they send out to the cake table to be sold. But the ones that have a chance at the prize they keep for final decision. They've kept mine so far, but Edith Holmes' was just sent out. It's too bad, it's a lovely chocolate cake."

"It is too bad," agreed Dotty, "but I don't believe a chocolate cake will take the prize, do you?"

"No, probably not," said Maisie. "Mine's a variety cake. What sort is yours?"

Dotty hesitated, for she well knew they had no cake in the committee room, but Dolly said: "We made up ours. We mixed things together that we never heard of combining before. It was mostly Dot's invention."

"But Dolly made the layers and did the icing," put in Dotty, unwilling to take all the credit.

"Sounds lovely," said Maisie, and then her attention was diverted elsewhere and she ran away.

No more embarrassing questions were asked, for every one assumed that Dotty and Dolly had given their cake to the committee when they arrived.

A dozen times during the afternoon they were asked, "Has your cake been sent out yet?" And they truthfully answered no.

But no hint could they glean from the words or looks of any girl to make them suspect wrong-doing.

"I can't keep it up any longer, Dot," said Dolly at last, in an undertone. "I feel as if I'm telling a lie, when I let them all think we have a cake with the committee."

"Fiddlesticks! it's none of their business. And anyway they have just that much more chance at the prize. Don't tell anybody, Doll, it can't do any harm to keep it to ourselves, and if one certain person takes the prize, I just want to see how she looks or what she says when I tell her our cake was stolen."

"Why, Dotty Rose! Do you mean to say you suspect anybody?"

"I don't say that; and I won't mention any name, even to you, but just you wait and see. They'll announce the prize winner at six o'clock and it's after five now."

So Dolly deferred to Dotty's wishes in the matter, and as there was much going on and plenty of diverting incidents, the hour slipped away and soon a whisper was passed around that the committee had made their choice.

Mrs. Van Zandt, the aristocratic and somewhat eccentric old lady who had offered the prize, came over to the cake table and smiled as she began her speech.

"It has been rather difficult," she said; "to decide among the beautiful and delicious cakes selected by the committee, for my final test. There were half a dozen at the last judging, that seemed equally well made and delightful of taste. Of course, I did not know who made the various entries, and so I decided, entirely on the merits of the cake itself. And considering everything, the method, the execution and the delicacy of flavours, I adjudge the best cake submitted in this contest to be the one that represents the joint work of Miss Dorothy Rose and Miss Dorinda Fayre. And I'm greatly pleased to present these two young ladies with the golden double eagle I offered as a prize, and I consider it well earned and honestly won."

If Dolly and Dotty had been amazed when they missed the cake from the pantry window, they were ten times more amazed now. What could it mean? There must be some mistake. Dotty's quick thought was that somehow their names had been connected with some other girl's cake, but in a moment that illusion was dispelled by the sight of their own beautiful white cake being brought in and placed in the very centre of the cake table.

It was positively their own cake, although a portion had been cut from one corner for the members of the committee to taste.

Realising that by some miracle their cake had been submitted, and had won the prize, Dolly and Dotty suddenly became aware that they must do their part, and together they stepped forward to receive the prize from Mrs. Van Zandt.

"I'm sorry it is not in two ten dollar gold pieces," she said, as she smilingly held it out to the blushing girls; "but you must divide it between you."

Smiling, Dolly and Dotty held out their hands together, and together received the gold piece, holding it between them as they bowed their thanks.

Then there was a hubbub of congratulations and laughter and chatter from the girls. It seemed unnecessary to say anything about the cake having been stolen, so the two D's smiled and beamed as they listened to flattering words about their prize winning cake.

Soon they were flying homeward to tell the family all about it.

"Our cake was there, and we took the prize!" cried Dotty, as they rushed into the living-room of the Rose bungalow.

"How did it get there?" cried Mrs. Rose, and Mr. Rose and Genie exclaimed in surprise, while Maria appeared in the kitchen doorway, holding up her hands and crying out: "Dem sperrits jes' nachelley wafted dat cake right ober to de fair place!"

"We don't know," Dolly went on, taking up the tale. "I asked two or three ladies of the committee, and they didn't seem to know anything about it—about how it got there. They just said it was there, entered in our names, and it sounded so silly to ask them to find out who brought it, that I just didn't."

"It was our cake," declared Dotty; "and it took the prize. So that's all right. But, however did it get there, unless it walked over itself. You didn't take it, did you, Daddy?"

"No," said Mr. Rose; "I did not. I would willingly have done so, but you girls insisted on taking it yourselves."

Just then the boys rushed in.

"Great sport!" cried Bob, flinging his cap and sweater on a chair; "Norris's boat is the swiftest thing ever!"

"You bet it is! Wow, but it was a great race!" And Bert Fayre waved his hands in enthusiasm; "Hello, girls, did your dinky white cake catch the gold piece? Did you bamboozle the judges into thinking it was fit to eat?"

"Yes, we did!" cried Dolly, her blue eyes sparkling with delight; "but, oh, Bert, what do you think! We don't know how the cake got there!"

"Got there? Why, Bob and I took it over. We knew you girls never could transport that masterpiece of modern architecture all that way in safety."

"You boys took it over?" and Dotty looked dumfounded.

"Sure we did," said Bob; "weren't you glad?"

"But why didn't you tell us? we almost went crazy!"

"Crazy nothing! We left a note on the pantry shelf saying we took it. We called to you girls but you were primping in your room and didn't answer. Maria wasn't on deck, so I just scribbled on a paper that we'd taken the cake and left the paper in its place."

Bob looked injured at the thought that their kindness was not appreciated.

"We didn't see any note," said Dolly; "where did you leave it?"

"Right on the pantry shelf, where we took the cake away from. You don't seem awful grateful, for what we thought would be a boon and a blessing to you. I can tell you we had to work pretty hard to get the old thing over there without a smooch on it, and I didn't dare put anything over it for fear it would stick to the icing."

While he was talking, Dotty had flown out to the pantry and returned with the bit of scribbled paper. "Here it is!" she cried; "it was on the floor under the shelf!"

"Must have blown off," said Bert, carelessly; "well, no harm done; cake got there all right. Took prize all right. Everybody happy."

"Yes, we are now," and Dolly grinned contentedly; "but we had a pretty miserable afternoon."

"Oh, pshaw, now," and Bob tweaked the black curls that clustered round her temple; "you must have known we took it, even without the note. Where else could it have gone to?"

"That's so," agreed Dotty; "and it's all right now. But next time you leave an important document for me, don't leave it in an open window on a breezy afternoon."

CHAPTER XVI

A WALK IN THE WOODS

"Only three days left of Camp Crosstrees," said Dolly, as the girls sat in the shack one summer afternoon. "I never knew two weeks to slip away so quickly."

"Don't you love it?" said Dotty, looking around at the various delights of camp life, the wooded hills and the distant mountains. "There's nothing like it, Doll; I wish we didn't ever have to go back to town."

"You'll have your visit with me, before we go back to Berwick. I wonder if you will like Surfwood, Dotty?"

"I'll love the seashore, I know; but I don't know about liking the big hotel. Don't you have to keep dressed up all the time and all that?"

"Why, we don't wear party clothes all the time. Of course we can't go around in an old serge skirt and middy blouse as we do here. But mornings we'll wear ginghams or linen frocks and late in the afternoon dress up nice."

"Awful bother, fixing up so. I like to go round as we do here. Nobody cares what they wear in camp."

"Of course it's awfully different at the hotel, but you'll like it after you get there. I don't see why you object to dressing decently. It's only a habit, going around in these old regimentals!"

Dolly looked with distaste at her brown serge skirt, and her tan stockings and shoes, the latter decidedly the worse for wear and scarred and scratched by stones and brambles.

"Oh, I've got plenty of good clothes; Mother's been fixing them all in order. And I know I'll like it to be down there two weeks with you. But I mean for a whole summer, I'd rather be up here, tramping around the woods and dressing like Sam Scratch, than to fuss up fancy every day."

"I wouldn't. I've had an awful good time up here on this visit, but for a whole summer, I'd rather be at the seashore, and at a hotel where I wear pretty white dresses and silk stockings and slippers."

"Aren't we different!" and Dotty laughed as she looked at her golden haired friend. "Sometimes I wonder, Doll, that we're such good friends, when we're so awfully different. Everything I like you hate and everything you like I hate."

"Oh, not quite that. In lots of ways, we like the same things."

"No, we don't. I like to go off in the woods on long tramps, and

113

you'd rather lie around here on a lot of balsam pillows and read a story book or do nothing at all."

"I expect I'm lazy."

"No, you're not, not a bit of it. You're ready enough to work if it's anything you like to do. Why, at a picnic, you'll do more than all the rest put together. We're just different, that's all. You're easy-going and good natured, and I'm a spitfire."

"Well, I guess it's good for us to be different, and so we influence each other, and that's good for both of us."

"Well, I'll influence you right now to go for a ramble in the woods. It's lovely to-day. Just the kind of a day when the breeze sings in the trees and the birds flutter low and you can watch them."

"All right, I'll go, if you don't go too far, nor walk too fast. We've only three days more up here, and we won't have many more chances to go woodsing, so come on."

"All right, we've a good long afternoon. You go ask Maria for some cookies and fruit, and I'll go tell Mother we're going. But don't let Genie know. We don't want her along to-day, for she gets tired in about an hour."

Dolly went in search of Maria, half sorry that Genie was excluded from the party, for unhampered by the child, Dotty was apt to walk fast and far in her untiring energy. But Dolly could always make her stop and rest by a reference to the weak muscles that still troubled her a little on a long walk. The girls had entirely recovered from their broken bones, but Dolly's was an indolent nature and disinclined to great exertion at any time.

Carrying their sweaters and a box of food they started off for their tramp in the woods.

"I want to get a whole lot of birch bark," Dolly said, as they walked along; "let's look for particularly nice pieces and get a whole lot to take with us down to the seashore."

"What for?"

"Oh, to make fancy work out of. Everybody does fancy work and they have bazaars, something like the one where we took the cake prize. And we can make lovely things out of birch bark for the bazaar tables."

"All right, we'll gather a heap. What shall we do with our cake prize, Doll, save it or spend it?"

"I'd rather spend it. I think it would be nice if we bought something special with it. Two things you know, just alike, to remember our first cake by."

"Something to wear?"

"Maybe. A ring or a pin or something."

"Couldn't get much of a ring for ten dollars. And we've got a lot of little fancy pins, both of us. What do you say to a gold pencil for each?"

"Only they never write very well; the leads are so hard."

"That's so. Well maybe beads, or how about a lace collar?"

"Let's wait till we get down to Surfwood and ask Trudy. She'll tell us something nice, and maybe we'll buy something there, or else in New York as we go through on the way down."

"All right. Here's some good birch bark, only it's yellowish. Let's keep on till we find some whiter."

The pair rambled on, happily chatting and laughing and now and then sitting down to rest or to refresh themselves from the box of lunch which was rapidly growing lighter.

"We have an awful lot of bark," said Dotty, looking at the big bundles they had collected.

"Yes, too much. Let's chuck out the worst pieces and just keep the best. And I'd like some more of that silvery kind. It's awful pretty combined with this dark yellow to make things."

"We want to get some big pieces. A portfolio of the silvery kind lined with yellow is lovely."

"Yes, with one corner turned back and a ribbon bow on it."

"Yes, or tied with sweet grass. There's a big tree on ahead. We can get some there, I'm sure."

"All right and there's another tree out there,—that's a dandy."

Eagerly they went on, absorbed in their fascinating quest. For the hunting of birch bark is ever enticing and lures one on to further treasures like a mirage.

"We can't carry another scrap," said Dolly, at last, laughing to see Dotty with her arms full of rolls of bark and more pieces gathered up in her skirt.

"No; we'll sit down and straighten this out and roll it up and finish the cookies and throw away the box and then we'll go home."

It was hard to throw away any of the beautiful bark, for they had gathered only fine specimens, and the quantity they finally selected to keep was a goodly load.

"We'll put on our sweaters," said Dolly; "so we can carry it all. It's no heavier than that lunch box was."

"No heavier," agreed Dotty; "but a good deal more bunglesome and awkward to carry."

Each girl had a big fat roll under each arm and turning they started gaily along in single file.

"You go first," said Dolly, stepping back; "I'm not sure I know the way. I declare to goodness, Dot, I don't see how you remember the way yourself. You've got a regular guide's brain under that black

115

mop of yours! How do you know which way to go, when you can't see anything but trees?"

"Easy as pie!" Dotty called back over her shoulder. "Just follow the nose of Dorothy Rose and away she goes!" And Dotty hopped over a big stone, while Dolly walked around it.

On they went, Dotty leading the way and Dolly following.

"It's getting awfully late, I believe the sun has set," said Dolly, shivering a little under her woollen sweater.

"Oh, no, the sun hasn't set, but you can't see it in these thick woods. We'll soon be out of this thick part now. We came quite a way in, Dollypops."

"A million miles, I should say! That's the worst of you, Dot, you never realise that all the walk you take has got to be walked back again!"

"'I took a walk around the block, to get some exercise,'" Dotty chanted, imitating a popular song which was a favourite with the boys.

"Exercise! I've had enough to last me the rest of the summer! Honest, Dot, I've got to rest a few minutes; I can't walk another step."

"Dollyrinda Fayre, you do give out the easiest of anybody I ever saw! Sit down on that stone and rest, do. But you mustn't wait long, for I guess it is about sunset. I feel sort of chilly, and I don't hear the birds much."

"All right, Dotsy, I'm rested now," and Dolly jumped up and walked on. She tired easily, but also a rest of a very few minutes made her ready to walk on again. She followed Dotty in silence for some distance and then said; "you're sure you do know the way, aren't you?"

"M—hmm," Dotty flung back over her shoulder and trudged on.

But Dolly noticed a difference in Dotty's attitude. She walked as quickly as before but she was not quite so alert. Also, she kept turning her head suddenly from side to side with a gesture of an inquisitive bird, a little uncertain which way to fly.

"You do know the way, don't you, Dotty?"

"'Course I do, Doll, don't be silly."

"How do you know it?"

"Just by instinct. I've been around these woods so much, I just kind of know the way home, even if I can't see out. Don't you see this kind of a trail? We just follow this and it brings us out right by our own camp."

"Are you sure?"

"Yes, I'm sure! What's the matter with you, Dolly?"

"Nothing; only it seems as if we'd walked as far since we've started for home as we did when we were going."

"So we have, nearly. Just a little farther now and we come into that clump of beech woods, don't you know? Where there aren't any birch trees, hardly."

"Yes, I know where you mean; but this doesn't look like it."

"'Cause we haven't got there yet, that's why. You wouldn't think birch bark would be so heavy; would you?"

"I don't mind it. Here give me one of your bundles; I'd just as lieve carry it as not. Give me the one out of your left wing. I know that one must be tired."

"'Deed I won't. You've got enough to carry. I'll throw my left hand bundle away before I let you lug it."

"Oh, don't throw it away! It's a shame, after we've taken such trouble to gather it. Do let me carry it, Dotty."

"No, sir, I won't do it! I don't mind it, anyway. Come on, Doll, let's hurry a little. Don't you think it's getting sort of dark?"

"Not dark, exactly, but dusky here under the trees."

"It isn't dusk, Dolly, it's dark! I mean, it's after sunset, and the real dark will settle down on us in a few minutes. I know more about these woods than you do, and I know we want to get along faster. We mustn't be in here when it gets really dark."

"But you said you knew the way, Dot," and Dolly's tone was anxious.

"I do, most always, but if we'd been on the right track we ought to have been out of the woods before this. I must have got turned around somehow."

Dotty stopped still and turned a despairing face toward Dolly.

"Good gracious, Dot, you don't mean we're lost!"

"I hope not that, but honest, I don't know which way to go."

"Why not go straight on?"

"I'm not sure, but I think that leads us deeper into the woods."

"Why, Dorothy Rose! You said that was the way home!"

"I know I did, and I thought it was; but don't you see, Dolly, if it had been the right way, we would be home by now?"

"Oh, Dotty, what are we going to do?"

Dolly's face took on a woe-begone expression, and her big blue eyes stared at the white face of her friend. "I'm frightened, Dolly, I— I never was lost in the woods before."

"Nor I, either. I've often heard of people being lost in these woods, when they were really quite near their homes. One man was lost for three days before they found him."

"Oh, don't say such dreadful things! It's getting awful dark, and I'm cold, and—and I'm scared!"

117

"I'm all those things, too! oh, Dolly, I'm awfully frightened!" and Dotty dropped her bundles of birch bark and sitting down on a stone began to cry hysterically.

Now Dolly Fayre was the sort to rise to an emergency, where Dotty Rose would lose her head completely. So Dolly, though terribly frightened, controlled herself, and sitting down, put her arm around Dotty and tried to cheer her.

"Brace up, Dot, it can't do a bit of good to cry you know. Now you know more about this sort of thing than I do, what do people do when they're lost in the woods?"

"Hol—holler," said Dotty, weakly, between her sobs, "holler like fury, and m-maybe somebody hears them and maybe they d-don't."

"All right, let's holler," and Dolly gave a yell, that sounded about as loud and carrying as the pipe or a bulfinch.

"Who do you s'pose'll hear that?" and Dotty almost smiled through her tears; "this is the way to holler." Dotty gave a loud scream, a long halloo, tapping her fingers against her mouth as she did so, making a peculiar mountain cry, known to campers.

"All right, I'll do that, too," and Dolly set up a rival yell.

But though both girls did their best, their screams were not very loud and they were followed by a silence, so intense, that they shivered and clung together in fear. The dark had fallen suddenly, and though only about seven o'clock, in the thick woods, they could scarcely see each other's faces.

Appalled by the awfulness of the situation, Dolly burst into tears, and though not as violent as Dotty's, her sobs were deep and racking ones.

"Oh, don't, Dollyrinda, don't cry so! I'll never forgive myself for losing you in these awful woods!"

"You didn't lose me, any more than I lost you. We both lost each other; I mean— I guess I mean we're both lost!" and Dolly's tears fell afresh.

Then both girls gave way and cried desperately, till they could cry no more, and with their stayed tears, they seemed to take a brighter outlook.

"If we're lost," said Dolly, philosophically; "we must make the best of it. Are there any wild animals, that would eat us up?"

"No, nothing of that sort. Nothing but squirrels and birds, and they can't hurt us."

"Then there's nothing really to be afraid of—"

"No, I s'pose not. Only starving to death, and catching pneumonia and a few little things like that."

"We won't starve right off, that's certain," said Dolly, practically; "at least I won't, I'm so fat. But you poor little picked chicken, you may!" And Dolly patted the thin little shivering shoulders that snuggled up against her.

"I'm hungry now; I wish we'd saved the cookies."

"You can't be hungry, Dot, not really hungry. Now, let's plan what to do. Shall we walk on and take our chances or shall we camp here for the night. It isn't so very different being here under the trees or under our own trees in camp."

"'Tisn't very different, hey? Well I think there's all the difference in the world! What are you going to sleep on? What are you going to cover yourself with? Oh, you know we couldn't sleep anyway, when we're lost!" and Dotty suddenly gave a vigorous yell which startled Dolly nearly out of her wits. But realising what it was for, she quickly joined in, and the two shrieked and shouted until it seemed to them that all the camps in that region must hear them.

But only those who have tried it, know how thoroughly one may get lost in the Adirondack woods in a very short time, or how loudly one may scream without being heard even by the friends who are searching for them.

And they were searching for the lost girls. When the two failed to appear by half-past six, Mr. and Mrs. Rose became apprehensive for their safety. They knew the girls had gone for a long ramble in the woods, but it was the rule of the camp to be back for six o'clock supper, unless due notice had been given.

"They're lost in the woods," Mrs. Rose declared, and though hoping the contrary, Mr. Rose agreed with her.

They had telephoned to all the neighbouring camps and as no one had seen the girls that afternoon they felt sure of what had happened.

"We must make search parties," said Bob, while Bert looked thoroughly scared at the thought of his sister's danger. "It isn't so awfully unusual, Bert. People get lost in the woods often, don't they, Dad?"

"Yes," replied Mr. Rose; "but it isn't often our little girls! Call up Long Sam, Bob; tell him to bring lanterns."

Many of the neighbours volunteered assistance and inside of an hour there were various search parties beating the woods for the missing girls.

But Dotty, when thinking she was walking toward home had really been walking in the opposite direction and the two girls were much farther away from camp than their rescuers thought for.

"Nothing doing," said Jack Norris, despondently, as he met Bob and Bert in the woods.

"Then we must keep at it," said Bert; "anything is better than giving up."

119

The various searchers separated and came together again. They screamed and shouted; they whistled and blew horns; their dogs barked, and it seemed as if some of these noises must reach the girls' ears and bring response calls.

But there was no success, and one by one the neighbours gave up and went home.

But Mr. Rose and the two boys, with Long Sam, kept up the search all through the night. They built fires occasionally, but dared not leave them, and put them out as they went on.

At last, Long Sam seated himself dejectedly on a fallen log, his extraordinary length of limb doubling up like a jacknife.

"'Tain't no use," he declared. "They ain't no livin' use o' trackin' these woods any longer. We mought strike them girls in a minute and then again we moughtn't run across 'em in a thousand years. Lord knows I'm willin' to keep on, but I'm jest about tuckered out. And I put it to you Mr. Rose, wouldn't it be better to rest a bit, and then push on?"

"Perhaps it would, Sam," and Mr. Rose's fingers worked nervously; "but I couldn't stay still, I'd go crazy. I think I'll push on and take my chances."

"Yes, and get yourself lost," grumbled Sam; "so's we'd have three to hunt 'stidden o' two!"

"You are done up, Sam," said Bert Fayre, kindly. "You stay here, and we three will drive ahead a little."

"Wal, I'll jest give one more howl, and see if that ketches anythin'."

Long Sam stood up on a log and gave a high pitched, long drawn out shout, that seemed as if it must penetrate the farthest depths of the forest.

"Now one, all together, like that," he said, and the four voices, joined in a mighty shout and then waited in breathless silence.

"I heard 'em!" Sam cried out; "I heard 'em! Now all you keep quiet!" And then Sam's voice rang out once more in a sharp short shriek. He listened and then exclaimed; "Yep! I heard 'em! Come on!" And with long strides he started anew into the blackness of the woods.

The others eagerly followed. They had heard no sound, but their ears had not the marvellous acuteness of the Adirondack guide, and without a word they hastened to keep up with Long Sam's pace.

"Sing out again!" Sam cried, several times, and at last the others could hear the faint high shrieks of Dotty and Dolly.

It seemed an endless journey, but at last the search party came upon the two girls.

"Oh, Father!" and Dotty threw herself into his arms, while Bert made a grab for Dolly and Bob danced around the group in glee.

"You're a nice pair!" observed Long Sam, who was no respecter of persons, when acting in his capacity of guide. "What d'you cut up such a trick as this for? You might 'a'knowed you'd get lost!"

"Now Sam, don't scold," said Dolly, well knowing that the bluff chap was really talking roughly to hide his glad emotion at the rescue.

"You ought to be scolded all the same, but I s'pose your folks is so glad to get you back that they'll just make the world and all of you."

And Sam's prognostication was verified. Following Sam's lead the party trudged through the woods, all so jubilant at the happy ending to their search, that scolding was not even thought of. And indeed why should it be? The girls had done nothing wrong, unless perhaps they had wandered a little deeper into the forest than it was advisable to go without a guide. But Dotty was positive it would never happen again. And when they reached camp and found Mrs. Rose and Genie waiting for them and a most appetising supper spread out by Maria, the two refugees found themselves looked down upon as heroines and were quite willing to accept the rôle.

CHAPTER XVII

SURFWOOD

A couple of days after their forest experience the two girls made ready to go to the seashore.

Secretly, Dolly was glad. She had enjoyed much of her stay at Camp Crosstrees, but she had about concluded that "roughing it" was not altogether to her taste. She had liked the gay parties round the camp fires, the swift motor-boat trips and the jolly picnic feasts, but she was not enthusiastically fond of long tramps up and down mountains and the deprivation of many home comforts and luxuries. She said no word of this to her kind hosts, but she welcomed the day that would take her back to her own people and their usual summer abode.

Also there had been really unpleasant experiences, from her lonely first night to that last awful night in the woods, and though these things were nobody's fault, they remained in Dolly's memory as decidedly undesirable pictures of her mountain trip.

Dotty Rose, all unconscious of Dolly's secret feelings, realised only that they had had lots of gay times together and many occasions of rollicking camp-life fun. Having spent many summers at Camp Crosstrees, the Rose family had become attached to the place, and always looked forward with eager anticipation to each successive trip.

Unlike Dolly, Bert Fayre loved it all. To him, roughing it was fun, and he cared nothing at all for the city comforts that were missing. He tramped the woods and went fishing, swimming and boating with the same enjoyment of these sports that Bob Rose felt, and he was more than delighted when Mrs. Rose invited him to spend the rest of August at the camp while the girls went for their two weeks at the seashore.

So on the day of departure Dotty and Dolly bade good-bye to their brothers and to Mrs. Rose and Genie, and in care of Mr. Rose started for New York and thence down to Surfwood, a resort on the New Jersey coast, where the Fayre family were staying at a hotel.

"Oh, don't you just hate to leave it?" exclaimed Dotty as the motor-boat took them swiftly down the lake. "Good-bye, you dear old woods; good-bye, you lovely lake. I shan't see you again till next summer."

For, as the children must begin school early in September, both families would return to Berwick in about a fortnight.

Dolly did not entirely share Dotty's enthusiasm, but she realised the wonderful beauty of the scene as she looked back at the lake with its wooded shores and hills rising to the high mountains.

"It is splendid!" she said, very honestly, as she gazed at the beautiful landscape. "I'm afraid, Dot, that you won't have a good time down at Surfwood. It's awfully different, you know."

"'Course I'll have a good time, if I'm visiting you. But, you see, we were a whole month later than usual coming up here this summer, and now to cut two weeks off the other end makes an awfully short season for dear old Crosstrees. Why do they call it Surfwood, Dolly; are there any woods there?"

"Yes, indeed; not far back from the beach there are lots of woods. But all flat, of course; no hills like these."

"Well, you couldn't expect mountains and seashore together. I know we'll have lovely times there, anyway I'd rather be with you than to stay up here."

The girls had become inseparable friends and their stay in camp together had strengthened the bonds and made them even more fond of each other than they had been as neighbours. They were very different, but they were learning to accept each other's differences, and in some ways they frequently influenced one another's tastes or opinions.

"Good-bye, old lake!" Dolly called out again, as the motor-boat neared its dock. "We'll see you next summer,—you will come up here again next summer, won't you, Dolly?"

"We'll see when next summer comes," returned Dolly, laughing. "Perhaps you won't like Surfwood a bit, and you won't want to go there next summer, and if you don't, of course I won't come up here. You look awfully well in that new suit, Dotty."

"Hope I do, for it doesn't feel very good. Collar's too stiff." Dotty wriggled with a feeling of discomfort that the first wearing of a new garment often brings. The girls both wore suits of blue serge, made similarly, but not exactly alike; Dotty's being trimmed with black satin and collar and cuffs of fine white embroidery, while Dotty's was enlivened by accessories of bright plaid silk and tiny gilt buttons.

The trip was a pleasant one, and they reached New York next morning in time for luncheon. This Mr. Rose gave them at an attractive restaurant and the girls greatly enjoyed the novel scenes of the Metropolis.

"I just love to eat in a restaurant, don't you?" said Dolly, as she lingered over her elaborate and complicated dessert.

"Yes, indeed; I love to look around and wonder who the people

123

are. Only they're all grownups. You don't see hardly any children or girls our age."

"No," said Mr. Rose, "a public restaurant is no place for kiddies, except on such an occasion as this, when I have to feed you somewhere. But since you're here, you may as well enjoy yourselves. Do you want some more little cakes?"

After due reflection, the girls concluded that they did, and the fascinating tray of French confections was again offered for their selection.

At the station where they were to take the train for Surfwood, Mr. Fayre met them.

"Well," he exclaimed. "So I am to take the responsibility of these two beautiful young ladies."

"Yes," rejoined Mr. Rose; "but I'm glad to tell you that they are not really difficult to manage. They have behaved most properly all day and honestly I hate to give them up. I know Camp Crosstrees will seem deserted and desolate without these two little rays of sunshine."

After affectionate leavetakings, Mr. Rose departed and the two girls went on with Mr. Fayre.

He was not of such a jolly nature as Mr. Rose, nor so inclined to talk with the children.

He placed them in adjoining chairs in the parlour car, and after supplying them with picture papers and candies, he seemed to consider his responsibilities at an end, and taking his own seat, immediately buried himself in his newspaper.

"Not much like the Adirondacks, is it?" said Dolly, as they whirled along through the flat landscapes of New Jersey.

"No, of course not; you wouldn't expect it. How soon do we see the ocean?"

"Very soon, now. We'll get to Surfwood about six, but we'll see the ocean long before then, there are so many beach stations."

As they neared Surfwood, Mr. Fayre threw aside his papers and looked out for the girls again. He was a most courteous man and politely assisted them with their various belongings, treating them more as grown ladies than as children.

"There they are!" he cried, as the train stopped at the picturesque little station and they spied a big motor car in which Mrs. Fayre and Trudy were sitting.

Trudy was looking lovely in her light summer costume and she warmly welcomed the travellers as they got into the motor.

"How brown you both are," said Mrs. Fayre, kissing the girls; "a nice healthy tan, and very becoming! Did you hate to leave your camp, Dotty? and I suppose you, too, Dolly, became a devotee of mountain life."

"We did have lovely times, Mother, and I expect Dot was sorry to give it up, but I persuaded her."

"You'll have lovely times here, too," promised Trudy, smiling at them; "I'll see to that."

The car stopped at the entrance to a very large hotel. The broad verandas were filled with people, gaily dressed, and gathered in laughing, chatting groups. Between them and the ocean was a broad boardwalk also filled with people.

"Come along, girls," said Mrs. Fayre, and Dotty and Dolly followed her across the veranda and into a large entrance hall. It was very beautiful, with glistening white and gold decorations, a thick moss-green velvet carpet and tall palms round the walls. Then followed a bewildering succession of gorgeous rooms, and finally they went up in an elevator.

"Here we are," and Mrs. Fayre led the two girls into a large and handsomely furnished suite.

"This is our general sitting room," she went on, "and this is your bedroom, right next to Trudy's."

They entered a large room, with two brass beds and attractive appointments of all sorts. The chairs and lounges were covered with gay chintz and there was a long deep window seat from which, across a balcony filled with flowers, they could see the ocean.

"How perfectly lovely!" cried Dotty; "not much like our little rooms at camp, Doll. Oh, I'm sure I shall be very happy here. It's awfully kind of you, Mrs. Fayre, to invite me."

"I'm very glad to have you, dear, and I only hope you'll enjoy it as much as Dolly did her stay with you. We can't give you the wild, free life of a mountain camp, but we're going to do all we can to interest and amuse you. But I'm not sure that you will like the plan for this evening. As your things aren't unpacked, I thought you two wouldn't dine downstairs with us to-night, but would have a nice little dinner sent up here and served in the sitting-room."

"Oh, goody!" cried Dolly; "that's a lot more fun. I don't feel like dressing up for dinner to-night and I think that's a lovely plan. Don't you, Dot?"

As a matter of fact, Dotty would have preferred to go downstairs, for she was impatient to see more of the big hotel and the gay people. But she politely acquiesced, and Mrs. Fayre bustled away, saying she would see them again after dinner.

"Now we'll have a lovely time, Dotsy, all to ourselves," Dolly said, as she flew around the room arranging things to suit herself.

A trim maid appeared to assist in any way needed, and the girls were glad to change their travelling clothes, and, after a refreshing bath, to don their pretty kimonos and boudoir caps, that Trudy had left in readiness for them.

"Trudy's a trump!" cried Dolly. "See these heavenly things she has laid out for us! A pink silk room-gown for you and a blue one for me, with caps to match. We share Trudy's bathroom, you see, so you can have this glass shelf for your things and I'll take this one for mine. I guess that's the dinner coming now, and then our trunks will come, and we can put our things away."

A very attractive little dinner was served in the sitting-room and the two girls sat down to it with a feeling as if they were "Playing house."

"We're to dine with the grownups after to-night," said Dolly; "new thing for me, 'cause always before I've had my supper in the children's dining-room. But Mother says, now I'm fifteen, I can always dine with them, unless they have special company and then we'll have ours up here like this. Isn't this salad good?"

"Perfectly lovely. But, somehow, I feel so queer. It's such a sudden change from the camp table and Maria's flap-jacks."

Dolly laughed. "Yes, it is different. But I like that, Dot, the sudden change I mean. Crosstrees was just right in every way for mountain and camp doings. Now this seashore stunt is altogether different, but I like this, too. And I think it's nice for us to have both kinds, one right after the other."

"So do I," said Dotty, as she contentedly ate her frozen pudding.

CHAPTER XVIII

DOLL OVERBOARD!

The next morning Dotty and Dolly went with the Fayre family to breakfast in the hotel dining-room.

Very fresh and pretty the girls looked, Dolly in a pale blue linen and Dotty in pink linen with a black velvet belt.

The great dining-room was large and airy, and the sunshine and sea breeze came in at the open windows.

The Fayres' table was pleasantly placed overlooking the ocean, and Dotty's black eyes roved round the room in delighted appreciation of the surroundings.

"Oh!" she exclaimed suddenly, "there are the twin Browns! Did you know they were here, Dolly?"

"I thought they would be; they come here 'most every summer." And Dolly smiled across the room at Tod and Tad, who bobbed their heads and grinned in response.

"I'm glad they're here," Dolly went on; "it's so nice to have some one you know to start you getting acquainted."

"It won't take you long to get acquainted," said Trudy, smiling, "for all the children of your age who are here are waiting for you. I've told several that you were coming, and I expect the Brown boys have made all sorts of plans for your entertainment. We won't bathe to-day until after luncheon; you can spend the morning on the beach or go for a motor ride with me, whichever you like."

As the girls hesitated over their decision, the Brown twins came over to their table and greeted them gaily.

"Thought you girls would never get here," said Tod, though really it mattered little which of them spoke, for they were so precisely alike it was impossible to tell them apart.

"Jolly to see you again," said Tad; "do come out on the beach with us as soon as you finish your breakfast, won't you?"

"Yes," said Dolly; "I guess we won't go with you, Trude, this morning; I want Dotty to get acquainted with the ocean."

And so when the girls left the dining-room, they found not only the Browns, but several other young people waiting on the veranda to escort them down to the beach.

There were general introductions, and as they went down the long flight of the hotel steps, Dolly found herself walking beside a girl named Pauline Clifton.

Pauline was rather tall and seemed to have an air of authority.

Though not exactly pretty, she was striking-looking, with brown eyes and hair and a complexion of rosy tan. She wore a white dress and a red sweater and white stockings with red shoes, and she put her hand through Dolly's arm with a decided air of possession.

"I like you already," she said, "and I'm sure we're going to be chums. Are you rich?"

The question struck Dolly as funny, and she turned to look into Pauline's face. But the brown eyes were serious, and evidently the Clifton girl wished an answer and was prepared to rate her new friend accordingly.

"No," said Dolly, returning the frank gaze; "we're not rich. We live in a small town, and we have about everything we want, but I'm sure we're not what you'd call rich. Are you?"

It would never have occurred to Dolly to ask this question, but it seemed to follow naturally after the other's.

"Oh, yes," Pauline said, "we're awfully rich. We live in New York, and my father has a yacht and lots of motor cars and everything."

"I should think you'd have your own summer home, then, and not come to a hotel."

"We have; two of them. One on Long Island and one up in the mountains. But Father takes freaks. I haven't any mother, and he jumps around wherever he feels like it. So he picked this place for August and here we are. There's only me and Carroll, that's my brother. He's that boy on ahead, with his cap on the back of his head."

"Who looks after you; your father?"

"Yes; but he isn't here much. We have a kind of a nurse-governess; that is, she used to be our nurse when we were little and she has always stayed with us. She's a funny old thing, Liza her name is, but she can manage us better than anybody else. Father tried a French governess for me and a German Fraülein, and Carroll has a different tutor about every month, but Liza just stays on through it all. I know all about you from the Brown boys. Aren't they ducks! They told us about you before you came, and about Dotty Rose. Isn't she pretty? You're awfully pretty, too, and you two look lovely together."

Pauline rattled on, scarcely giving Dolly a chance to reply to her observations. Meantime the group had come to a standstill and were selecting a nice place on the beach to spend the morning hours.

Dotty was enchanted with her first real experience of the seashore.

She sat down in the sand with the rest, but quickly made her way to the front of the group and as near as possible to the edge of

128

the waves in her effort to get an unobstructed view of the ocean. The surf was rolling in and the great breakers filled her with awe and delight.

"Come farther back, Dotty," Tad Brown called out, "or you'll get caught by some of those swells."

Dotty drew back just in time to escape a wetting from a big wave whose white foam rolled up the sands to her very feet.

"Isn't it wonderful!" she cried; "I could sit right here all day and never take my eyes off those waves!"

But the sight was not so novel to the others, and they talked and laughed and threw sand at each other and built forts and watched for passing steamers and made plans for future amusements.

"That's the worst of the seashore," said Pauline, discontentedly; "there's so little to do. Just walk the boardwalk or sit on the sand or bathe; that's about all."

"Nonsense, Polly," said her brother Carroll; "there's lots else to do. Going motoring or walking in the woods, and there's a bowling alley at the hotel and tennis courts—there's millions of things to do, only you're such an old grouch you never see the fun of anything."

Pauline paid no attention to this brotherly remark, but said to Dotty, "Come on, let's go for a walk; I want to get acquainted with you."

"Get acquainted here," said Dotty, laughing. "I'm too comfortable to move."

The Brown boys had banked up a big hill of sand behind Dotty, and she leaned back against it, still fascinated by the wonderful blue of the distant ocean sparkling in the sunlight and the mad onrush of the great breakers as they dashed on the shore.

"Then you come," said Pauline to Dolly; "let's go off by ourselves and walk along toward the casino and the shops.

"All right," said Dolly, who was tired of sitting on the sand and quite ready for a walk. Moreover, she was curious to know more of Pauline. She wasn't sure she should like a girl who asked her point blank if she were rich, and yet Pauline didn't seem ostentatious or vulgar, but was quick-witted and full of fun.

The two walked away, leaving the rest of the crowd, some six or eight of them, on the beach.

As the morning passed, others joined the group and some went away, but Dotty remained, still unable to tear herself away from the glorious sea.

"I say, Dot Rose," Tod Brown exclaimed, "you are stuck on that big pond, aren't you? But there are other days coming when you can gaze at it. Come on, now, and let's do something. I'll race you to the end of boardwalk."

"What's there, when you get to the end?" demanded Dotty.

"Nothing much, but some fishermen's shacks and nets and things. Come on and see it. The fishermen are a queer-looking bunch and not very good-natured, but it's fun to tease them. Come on, anyhow."

Dotty got up, somewhat cramped by long sitting, and was glad after all for a brisk walk in the sunshine. They didn't race, but swung along at a good pace, Dotty with her eyes still seaward.

Nearly at the end of the boardwalk, on a bench, was a large and handsome French doll. It was dressed as a baby, with a long white frock, a lacy cap and a knitted pink sacque.

"Oh, look at that!" cried Dotty. "I know whose it is; it belongs to that little golden-haired child at the hotel."

"That's so," said Tod. "The kiddy must have left it here. I saw her lugging it around this morning, and it was about all she could do to carry it. Shall we take it back to her?"

"Yes," said Dotty; "I'd just as lieve carry it."

"You bet you'll carry it, if either of us does. Do you s'pose I'd go round lugging a wax infant?"

"It isn't wax," said Dotty, picking it up; "it's light as a feather. It's one of those celluloid things, but I never saw such a big one before. Yes, I'll take it back to little Yellowtop. If it's left here somebody will steal it. Shall we turn back now?"

"No; come on to the end of the walk and let's have a look at the fishermen."

They went on and soon reached their destination. It was a picturesque place, but the cabins were deserted and only a few empty boats were in sight. The beach was littered with old fish nets and various sorts of rubbish, while a few piers ran out into the sea.

"Everybody's gone fishing," said Tod. "Nothing much to see here; let's go back."

"Let's go out to the end of that pier," said Dotty. "There's no danger, is there?"

"Danger? No! But nothing to see out there. Come along, though, if you like."

Good-naturedly, Tod went with Dotty along the old pier. Reaching the very end, they sat down for a few moments, their feet hanging over the edge while they clung to the uprights.

"Oh, isn't it grand!" cried Dotty, looking down into the blue water as it rippled against the piles at some distance below.

"Don't fall in," warned Tod.

"Never fear, I'm not that kind of a goose! I love it, but I'm scared to death all the time, and I keep a good grip on this rope."

"That's right. Oh, here comes a fishing-boat; see, 'way out there in the distance. We'll wait for that to get in, and then we'll go."

The two stood up, and hanging onto the ropes, leaned far over to see the boat as it came in.

A sudden breeze made Dotty cling closer to the upright she was leaning against, and as Tod put out his hand to steady her, somehow or other the big doll dropped into the water.

"Oh, my goodness!" exclaimed Dotty in dismay, "there goes the baby's doll! What a pity. Can we get it, Tod?"

"I don't know. If it doesn't drift the wrong way, maybe the fishermen will pick it up as they come in. If I had a hook and line I could hook it up."

"Don't lean over so far, Tod; you'll fall in," and Dotty tried to hold back the boy as he leaned over the edge of the pier. "Oh, see, there's a fisherman or somebody, coming out of that cabin. Maybe he'll bring a pole or something and help us get the doll. Ask him to."

Tod shouted at the man, who had just appeared in the cabin door. It was some distance and the boy's voice did not carry well over the breakers between them, but finally Tod succeeded in attracting the man's attention.

"Bring a pole!" Tod shouted, "or fish line. Help us!"

"Hey?" shouted the man, his hand to his ear. "What's the matter?"

"Doll overboard!" Tod yelled back, but the breeze was off shore and the man could not get the words. But he saw the two children as they pointed out on the water, and then, as he saw the big doll, he very naturally thought it was a live baby and immediately he became excited. He ran back into the cabin and returned with a boat-hook. He jumped into a boat and endeavoured to put out to sea through the breakers. But at every attempt, the waves dashed him back on the shore. Determinedly, he tried again and again, and finally succeeded in getting beyond the surf, though he was now at some distance from the pier. He began to row desperately, but made little headway toward the floating doll.

"He thinks it's a live baby!" cried Tod, roaring with laughter. "Oh, Dotty, what a joke! Keep it up! Pretend it is."

Willingly enough, Dotty caught at the idea and began wringing her hands and screaming frantically.

"Oh, save her, save her!" she yelled, tearing around the pier like a mad person, while Tod, hanging on to a post, leaned far over the water and waved his hand frantically to the boatman.

The fisherman redoubled his efforts and slowly drew nearer the floating doll, whose long white dress was whirled and tossed about in the eddy.

131

The boatload of fishermen which they had seen in the distance drew nearer, and the man in the row-boat communicated to them by shouts and signs and made them aware of the catastrophe.

The incoming fishermen saw the baby in the water, and saw the two children screaming and wailing on the pier, and they put forward with all speed to make a rescue.

Tod and Dotty were really doubled up with laughter, but pretended they were in agonies of grief as the two boats made desperate attempts to reach the drowning child.

"The old idiots!" exclaimed Tod; "they might know that a live baby wouldn't float around like that. It would have sunk long ago."

"Of course it would," agreed Dotty. "Won't they be mad when they get it!"

The fishermen, having had little experience with French dolls the size of live babies, assumed, of course, that it was a real child in the water, and they wasted no time in marvelling as to why it should continue to ride blithely on top of the waves. They simply put forth every effort to reach the white object, whatever it might be, but the perversity of wind and wave continued to thwart them.

At last, however, very near shore, the fishermen drew near enough to grab the doll and draw it into their boat, just as they rowed in on top of a huge breaker and beached near the pier.

Tod and Dotty ran swiftly to them, eager to see their chagrin and dismay at having rescued the doll.

The men were all out on the beach and they showed a belligerent demeanour as the children appeared.

"Ye little wretches," cried one big rawboned man, "what d'ye mean by foolin' us like that?"

His manner even more than his words were distinctly threatening, and Dotty was scared, but Tod answered him directly.

"We didn't fool you! We dropped the doll in the water by accident, and we sung out there was a doll overboard and we asked a man on shore to help us get it. If you people thought it was a live baby, that isn't our fault!"

"That don't go down!" and another man stepped forward and shook his fist at the children. "Ye know right well ye fooled us a-purpose."

"We did not!" and Dotty, her temper now aroused, stamped her foot at him. "We told the man it was a doll, but if he couldn't hear us, we couldn't help that."

"Now, now, little lady, ye know better." The big brawny fisherman came nearer to Dotty and scowled at her. "I seen you jumping around there and play-actin' like you was wild with grief! Don't deny it, now! Ye know well enough I say true!"

He glowered at Dotty, and as he came nearer to her his big fierce eyes frightened her and she quickly stepped behind Tod.

"Don't you speak to the lady like that!" the boy cried. "If you've anything to say, say it to me. I called to the man for help to get that doll out of the water. It belongs to a little friend of ours and we want to take it to her."

"Well, ye'll never take it!" and the fierce-eyed man picked up the wet and dripping doll, and with a mighty sweep of his long arm, he flung it far out to sea. The deed was merely an impulse of his angry wrath at having been fooled by the children, and he faced them with a defiant air.

"You had no right to do that!" cried Tod; "go right out in your boat and get it."

"Ha! ha!" laughed the man with a loud, boisterous chuckle. "Go out and get it, is it? Not much I'll not go out and get it! And, what's more, I'll report you two to the life-saving station people, and I'll have you arrested for false pretences."

Tod was pretty sure that this was all a bluff, but the other men gathered about and promised the same thing. So threatening were they, that Dotty was thoroughly scared, and Tod, though not really afraid of arrest, began to think that these men could make things very unpleasant for them. He knew by hearsay of the rough manners and ugly tempers of this particular lot of fishermen. He had heard stories of their dislike for the summer guests, who sometimes visited them out of curiosity and looked upon them patronisingly.

Tod realised that nothing incensed their rough natures like being made the subject of a practical joke and this, though unpremeditatedly, he and Dotty had done. He thought best to drop his indignant air and try to propitiate them.

"Oh, come now," he said; "honest Injun, as man to man, I didn't mean to fool you. We dropped the doll in the water and I yelled for help. Now, I'll own up that when you fellows seemed to think it was a live baby, we did kind of help along a little but we didn't mean any harm. S'pose I give you a dollar to forget it."

Tod spoke in a frank and manly way, and his good-natured face ought to have evoked a pleasant response. And it did from most of the men, but the fierce black-eyed one, who seemed to be the leader, was possessed of a sense of greed, and his one idea regarding the "stuck-up summer people" was to extract money from them whenever possible.

"A dollar," he said, with an unpleasant sneer; "not enough, young sir! Show us ten dollars, and we'll try to forget the insult you offered us."

133

"I didn't offer you an insult, and I haven't ten dollars with me, and I wouldn't pay it to you if I had!"

Tod was angry now, and his eyes blazed at the rude injustice of the demand.

But the fierce-browed man was not abashed. "You gimme ten dollars or I'll make trouble for you! If you haven't got it, you can get it. Gimme your word of honour—you look like a gentleman—to bring me that ten, and I'll promise to make no trouble."

Tod hesitated. Had he been alone, he would have refused them at once, but he felt that he had the responsibility of Dotty's welfare, and he paused to reflect. The men were very rude and uncontrolled, and Tod didn't know what further menace they might offer.

As he hesitated, the big man spoke more threateningly. "Be quick, young man; give us your word, or we'll put you under lock and key for awhile to think it over."

This speech was accompanied by growls of assent from other members of the group, and one or two stepped forward as if to carry out the suggestion.

CHAPTER XIX

SPENDING THE PRIZE MONEY

"Hoo—hoo!" called a gay voice, and Tod and Dotty turned to see Dolly Fayre flying toward them. She was alone and out of breath from running, but laughing gaily as she joined them.

"I ran away from Tad," she cried. "He went to get some candy, and just for fun, I scooted off. And somebody had said you came this way, Dot, so I followed just for fun. Why, what's the matter?"

Dolly looked in amazement at the group of angry men and at the half-frightened, half-indignant faces of Dotty and Tod.

"Matter enough," Tod said; "you keep out of it, Dolly. In fact, you girls go back to the hotel and leave me to fix things up with these men." Then he suddenly remembered his desire for an amicable settlement, and he said pleasantly, "I guess we can come to terms after the ladies have gone."

"I guess we can't!" said the black-browed man, in a surly tone. "You go back to the hotel, young man, and get that ten dollars, and I'll keep the young ladies here safe until you come back."

"Not much I won't!" cried Tod angrily. "Run on back, girls. Go on—beat it!"

"No, you don't!" and the big man stepped forward and laid his hand on Dotty's shoulder.

"Take your hand off that lady! Don't you dare to touch her," and Tod's eyes blazed as he flung himself toward the big man.

"What is it all about? What is the matter?" exclaimed Dolly, who couldn't understand what she had supposed was a good-natured chat with the fishermen.

"They want us to pay ten dollars," said Dotty, indignantly, "and unless we do, they're going to lock us up."

"Lock us up nothing!" shouted Tod, who was unable to decide himself what was the best thing to do. The arrival of Dolly had complicated his dilemma, for now he had two girls to protect instead of one. He wished Tad had come with her, for the twins were big and brawny for their years and could have made a fair showing of rebellion against the injustice of the fishermen.

Dolly considered the matter gravely. She looked from Dotty and Tod to the rude, unkempt men, and after a few moments' thought she made up her mind. Deliberately she opened a little chatelaine bag that hung at her belt and took from it a ten dollar gold piece. It was her share of the cake prize, for Mr. Rose had changed the twenty dollar gold piece into two tens for the girls.

She looked at the big man with scorn, and holding out the gold piece, she said in cool, haughty tones, "Here is your money; please do not detain my friends any longer."

"Don't you do it, Dolly," cried Tod; "it's an outrage!"

"I know it's an outrage," Dolly said, calmly, "but I prefer to pay the money rather than parley with these people."

Dolly's air of superiority would have been funny, had not all concerned been so deeply in earnest.

"Hoity-Toity!" said the big, ugly man, "you're a fine young miss, you are! You treat us like the dirt under your feet, do you? Well, if so be's you pay our claim, we ain't objectin' to your manner. Be as high and mighty as you like, but give us that there coin."

Without a further word, Dolly dropped the gold piece into the man's grimy, outstretched hand, and the three turned and walked away back to civilisation.

"I'm up and down sorry that I couldn't get you out of that mess better," said Tod, as they went along the boardwalk. "Of course, I'll pay you back the money, Dolly, only I felt mighty cheap to have you advance it. But I had only three or four dollars with me, not expecting a hold-up this morning."

"I don't think you ought to have paid it, Doll," said Dotty.

"'Tisn't a question of ought to," said Tod, seriously. "That's a rough, bad gang. I've heard of them before. I don't know what's the matter with them, but they're grouchy. All the other fishermen around here are fairly good-natured, but this lot is noted for ugly temper and they especially dislike and resent the summer people. I forgot all this, and of course Dotty didn't know it. But I didn't think, and when they supposed the baby was alive, I went ahead with the game without realising it meant trouble."

"Well, it's all right now," said Dolly, "and I was glad enough to give up my ten to ransom you two captives. Of course you won't pay it back to me, Tod, but you can each pay me a third of it and that'll square us all up."

"We'll each pay half," said Dotty, "there's no reason you should pay anything, Doll. You weren't in on this game. And here's another thing, I'm going to buy a new doll for that little girl. You see it's the same as if I stole hers."

"Not at all," said Tod. "She had lost her doll, anyhow. She must have left it there on the bench, and if we hadn't picked it up, somebody would have stolen it sooner or later."

"We can't be sure of that," said Dotty. "And anyway I took her doll, and I lost it for her, and it's up to me to get her another. And that's all there is about that. I've got my gold piece with me, too, and I'm going straight down to the shop and get the doll now."

Dotty was determined, and so the three went to the shop. There was only one place in Surfwood where toys and fancy goods were sold. But this shop was stocked with a high grade of goods and Dotty had no trouble in finding a doll nearly like the one which was now doubtless afloat on the wide ocean. The doll cost five dollars, but Dotty persisted in buying it, as she declared her conscience would never be easy unless she did.

"Now let's settle this thing up," said Tod, as they emerged from the store. "I find I have as much as five dollars with me, counting chicken feed, and I'll pay this to you, Dolly, as my half of the ransom you put up."

"And here's my five," said Dotty, handing over the bill she had received in change for the doll.

Dolly looked dismayed. "Why, good gracious, Dot, then here am I with ten dollars, and you with nothing of our prize money! I won't stand that for a minute, you take this five back, and then we'll be even all round. I rather guess if you get in a scrape like that, I've got a right to help you out."

"Well, I rather guess," said Tod, "that when we tell our folks about this matter there'll be something doing. I think those men ought to be shown up and punished."

"Oh, no," said Dolly. "They're an awful gang. I've heard Father say so, and I'm sure it's better to let them alone than to stir up any further trouble."

And as it turned out the elders concerned in the matter shared Dolly's opinion.

The story was told and Mr. Fayre and Mr. Brown talked over the matter and said they would take it in charge and the children need think no more about it, but they were directed to keep away from that locality in the future and confine their escapades to such portions of the beach and the boardwalk as were inhabited by civilised crowds.

Money matters were straightened out in a way acceptable to all concerned, by the simple method of the two fathers' remuneration of all that had been paid out, and so Dolly, Dotty and Tod found themselves possessed of the same finances they had before the unfortunate episode occurred.

"Dat not my dolly," declared the Chrysanthemum-headed baby, shaking her yellow curls as Dotty offered her the new doll.

"I know it," Dotty said, smiling as she knelt beside the child; "but let me tell you. I found your dolly sitting all alone on a bench, and I was going to bring her home to you. And then,—well, and

137

then, do you know that dolly went out to sea, way out to sea—and I think she's going to Europe as fast as she can get there. And so, I've brought you this other dolly, which is just as pretty."

Goldenhead looked up into the smiling black eyes, and after a moment's hesitation agreed that the new dolly was just as pretty as the departed one, and graciously accepted it.

Goldenhead's mother demurred at the whole transaction, but Mrs. Fayre insisted that the child accept the new dolly and so the matter was settled.

"Tell me everything all about it!" cried Pauline Clifton, rushing to meet the two D's on the hotel veranda. "Wasn't it thrilling? Such an experience! My, I wish I had been with you! And Tod Brown was perfectly fine, a real hero!"

"Didn't do a thing," growled Tod, and Tad who was beside him, said, "Wish I'd been there! then we could have sent the girls flying home and stood up to those toughs!"

"Aren't you splendid!" cried Pauline, but Dolly said, in her practical way, "It wouldn't have been splendid at all, it would have been very foolish for you two boys to think of fighting that crowd of great ugly men! It was a case, where the only thing to do, was to submit to their demand and come away. My father says we did just right."

"Of course, it was the only thing to do," said Tod, "but to me it seemed awful galling."

"Well, we'll never go there again," said Dotty; "and it ought to be a lesson to us not to play jokes on people."

"A lesson that you'll never learn," said Dolly, laughing; "you'll have to have worse experiences than that, Dotty Rose, before you stop playing jokes on people."

"Is that so?" cried Carroll Clifton; "then you're a girl after my own heart. I love to play jokes. Let's put our heads together and work up a good one on somebody."

"Well, this joke isn't on us, anyway," said Dotty, laughing. "We have our ten dollars back again, Dolly, and I say we spend them before we get a chance to lose them again."

"But we're going to spend those for something special. You know they are our cake prizes."

"Oho!" cried Carroll, "did you girls take a prize at a cake walk?"

"Not a cake walk, but we took a prize for making cake," Dotty exclaimed; "and I say, Dolly, let's buy something in that shop where we bought the doll. They have beautiful things there of all sorts."

"Come on," said Pauline, "let's all go, and we'll help you pick out things."

So the two Cliftons and the two Browns and the two D's all

started for the shop. It was that sort of summer resort bazaar that holds all kinds of fancy knick-knacks for frivolous purchasers.

"Going to get things alike or different?" asked Tod Brown, as they went in.

"Different, of course," said Tad, "Dot and Dolly never like things alike."

"Don't you really?" said Pauline; "how funny! I thought you were such great friends you always had everything just alike."

"No," said Dolly, "we have everything just different. You see our tastes are just about opposite, I expect that's why we're such friends."

Dotty and Carroll were already studying the things at the jewellery counter, while Dolly was slowly but surely making toward the book department.

"Get a picture," suggested Tad, "here are some good water colours of the sea."

"And here's a coloured photograph of that very fishing place where you were at," said Pauline.

All sorts of ridiculous suggestions were made, and the boys offered jumping-jacks and comical toys to the two spenders.

"Why don't you get a lot of little things, instead of one big thing?" said Pauline; "here are some darling slipper buckles, and I think these little flower vases are lovely."

"No," said Dotty, decidedly, "we're each going to get one thing and spend the whole ten dollars for it. And it must be something that we can keep and use."

"I've made up my mind," said Dolly, calmly; "I'm just looking around for fun, but I know perfectly well what I'm going to get. Do you, Dotty?"

"Yes, of course. I decided before I was in the store a minute."

"What?" chorused the others.

"This is mine," and Dotty went back to the jewellery counter and pointed out a silver-gilt vanity-case.

"Well, of all ridiculous things!" cried Tod; "you might as well have let the fishermen keep your money!"

"'Tisn't ridiculous at all!" Dotty retorted. "Mother told me I could get exactly what I wanted, and I want this dreadfully. I've wanted one for a long time. Don't you think it's pretty, Pauline?"

"Yes," returned Pauline, carelessly. "I have two of them, one real gold and one silver. But I hardly ever carry them."

"Oh, well, you can have whatever you want," said Dotty, good-naturedly; "but this is a treat to me, and I think it's lovely, though of course not grand like yours."

So Dotty bought the vanity-case, and then the crowd followed Dolly to see what might be her choice.

Straight to the bookshelves she went, and pointed to a set of fairy stories. They were half a dozen or more volumes bound in various colours and the set was ten dollars.

"I've been just crazy for these books," she said, with a sigh of satisfaction. "I would have had them for my birthday, only we had our rooms fixed up; and the minute I spotted them I knew I should buy them."

"What a foolishness!" exclaimed Carroll; "how can you read fairy tales?"

"She loves them," said Dotty; "she'd rather read a fairy story than go to a party, any day."

Dolly laughed and dimpled, but stuck to her decision and soon the crowd left the shop, carrying the important purchases with them.

Back at the hotel, they were exhibited, and Mrs. Fayre and Trudy smiled a little at the selection, but said they were glad that the girls had bought what they wanted.

CHAPTER XX

GOOD-BYE, SUMMER!

Days at Surfwood passed happily and swiftly. Dolly and Dotty often discussed the matter and always agreed that camp life and hotel life were equally pleasant, though in opposite ways. And if Dotty sometimes sighed for the careless freedom of the life in the woods or if Dolly felt in her secret heart that she preferred the more formal conventions of the big hotel, they soon forgot such thoughts in the joys of the moment.

There was seabathing every day and automobile trips and all sorts of beach fun and frolic.

The time was drawing near for them to go back to Berwick and settle down again to the routine of home life.

Among the last of the season's gaieties there was to be a children's dance in the big ball-room. This was a regular summer feature and all the guests of the hotel did their best to make the occasion attractive.

All under sixteen were considered children, and even some of the little tots were allowed to attend the festival. Fancy dress was not obligatory, but many of the young people chose to wear gay costumes.

The two Cliftons, the Brown twins and Dolly and Dotty had come to be a clique by themselves, and were always together.

"Let's dress alike for the silly party," said Clifford, who liked to appear scornful of such amusements, but who was really very fond of them.

"All right; how shall we dress?" said Dotty, who was always ready for dressing up.

"A shepherdess costume is the prettiest thing you can wear," said Pauline. "I have one with me, and it's lovely. S'pose you two girls copy that, and then have the boys rig up something like it."

"Mother will make us any old togs we want," said Tad, "It isn't a masquerade, is it?"

"Oh, no," said Dolly; "just fancy dress, you know, if you choose, and lots of them just wear regular party clothes."

"I'd like to be a shepherdess, all right," said Tad with a comical simpering smile.

"Now don't you make fun of my plan!" said Pauline; "we three girls can be shepherdesses, and you three boys can be shepherds. Shepherd lads are lovely, with pipes and things."

"Clay pipes?" asked Tod.

"No, goosy; pipes to play on. Long ones with ribbons; oh, 'twill be lovely!" and Pauline clapped her hands. "Liza will make you a suit, Carroll, and then the other boys can have it copied."

There was much further discussion and the elders were called into consultation, but finally Pauline's plan was adopted.

Her shepherdess' frock was dainty and beautiful. The Dresden flowered overdress was of silk, looped above a quilted satin petticoat, and a black velvet bodice laced up over a fine white muslin chemisette. A broad brimmed hat with roses and a be-ribboned shepherdess' crook completed the picture.

"It's perfectly lovely, Pauline," said Trudy, when she saw the dress, "but we'll copy it for the girls in less expensive materials. Flowered organdy will be very pretty for the panniers, and sateen or silkoline will do for the skirts. The hats can be easily managed, and I'm sure we can get the crooks down at the shop; if not, Dad will bring them from New York."

"You're a brick, Trudy," and Dotty flung her arms around the kind-hearted girl. "It's awful good of you to do mine as well as Dolly's."

"Oh, Mother will help me, and it'll be easy as anything. I love to do it."

Long suffering Liza was accustomed to do as she was told, so she set to work to evolve a shepherd costume for Carroll. She was skilful with her needle and out of sateen and some gay ribbons she constructed a suit that was picturesque and jaunty even if not entirely the sort a shepherd lad might choose for daily wear.

A soft white silk shirt with a broad open collar and a soft silk tie was very becoming to good-looking Carroll, and the pipes, so necessary to the character, were bought in New York by Carroll's father.

Mrs. Brown was quite willing to have this suit copied for her twins, and Tod and Tad, though growling at the idea of being "dressed up like Jack Puddings," were secretly rather pleased with the becoming garb.

"Suppose we make the caps for the boys," said Pauline, "I know just how and I think 'twill be fun."

The others agreed, and the day before the dance, the three girls pre-empted a cosy corner of the big veranda and sat down to work.

Copying a picture, it was not difficult to make the type of cap that would harmonise with the shepherds' suits.

Pauline cut them out and each of the girls sewed one.

"You haven't made the head-bands big enough, Pauline," said Dolly, as she tried an unfinished cap on her own curly head.

"They're plenty big enough," Pauline retorted, "the boys haven't such a mop of hair as you have."

"I know that; but even allowing for that I don't think they could ever get their heads into these small bands. Where are they, let's fit them on them."

"They've gone off for the morning. I tell you, Dolly, these bands are all right. Don't you s'pose I know anything? Of course I measured them before I began. Some people think they know it all!"

Pauline was quick-tempered and Dolly was not, so the latter made no response to the somewhat rude speech, and the girls sewed a few moments in silence.

Then as Dotty began to sew her cap to its band, she echoed Dolly's words: "Why, Polly, these bands aren't big enough, that's so!" and Dotty tried to put the cap on her own head.

"How silly you are!" exclaimed Pauline, angrily. "Do you suppose your head with all that hair isn't bigger than the boys' heads without any hair to speak of? I tell you I measured these bands and they're plenty big enough. If you girls want to be so disagreeable about it, you can make the caps yourselves."

"It's no use finishing these things," declared Dotty, "for the boys can't get their heads into them! Why they're hardly big enough for a six year old kid!"

"I tell you they are. I guess I know. I measured one on my own brother and his head is just as big as the Browns' heads are."

"You've got the big-head yourself!" Dotty flashed back at her, "you think you know everything, Pauline Clifton! I'm just sure the boys can't wear these caps, but we'll go on and finish them, since you say they're big enough."

"They are big enough! there's no reason why we shouldn't finish them!" and Pauline's cheeks grew red as she sewed hurriedly on the cap she held.

"Well, don't let's quarrel about it," said Dolly, who had not changed her opinion, but who wanted to make peace. "If Pauline says they're all right, Dotty, let's go on and sew them. She must know, if she measured Carroll's head."

"Of course I know!" and Pauline scowled at the other two girls. "If you'd sew instead of fussing and finding fault, we could get the things done before luncheon."

"All right," and Dolly smiled pleasantly, shaking her head at Dotty, who was just about to make an angry speech. "If Polly takes the responsibility, I'm satisfied to go on, but it certainly doesn't seem to me that any boy could get his head into that thing!" And she held up a cap whose head band certainly did seem small.

"I'll take the responsibility all right," and Pauline shook her head angrily. "And when you see the boys with these caps on, you'll realise how silly you've acted."

The girls stitched on for a few minutes without speaking and then Dolly's gentle voice broke the silence with some comment on some other subject and peace was restored outwardly, though each of the three was conscious of an angry undercurrent to their conversation.

The caps finished, Pauline took the three of them and said she would give them to Liza, who had the ribbon streamers for them.

So the trio separated and as the Fayres had an engagement for that afternoon the three girls were not together again until the next day.

The next day was the day of the dance, but there was a tennis tournament in the afternoon, in which all the young people took part, and so interested were they in the games that no reference was made to the quarrel of the day before.

The dance was in the evening, and at dinner time Dolly and Dotty passed the Cliftons' table on their way to their own.

"Get dressed early and come down to the ball-room as soon as you can," Carroll said to them as they went by. "The party is a short one, anyway."

The children's dance was only from eight till ten as the more grown-up young people claimed the floor later.

Trudy helped Dolly and Dotty into their pretty dresses and both she and Mrs. Fayre exclaimed with admiration.

The costumes of organdy and sateen were quite as pretty as the model of silk and satin. Both girls wore their hair hanging in loose curls and their broad rose-trimmed hats had long streamers of blue and pink ribbon which tied under the chin with a bow at one side. Their long white crooks bore bunches of ribbon and each carried a little basket of flowers to add to the dainty effect.

They found the others awaiting them in the ball-room, and indeed the dancing was just about to begin as they arrived.

It was a pretty sight. The long handsome room was specially decorated with flowers and banners, and the gaily dressed children were laughing and running about in glee. Many of eight or nine, were dancing in pretty fashion, and indeed all ages under sixteen were represented. This frolic was an annual affair and the majority of the children staying at the hotel were allowed to attend.

Perhaps half of them were in fancy costume and fairies and Red Ridinghoods flitted about with Bobby Shaftos or miniature cavaliers.

"Isn't it beautiful!" cried Dotty, at the threshold of the ball-room. She had never seen a party just like this before and the gay sight entranced her.

"We can't go in," laughed Trudy, as she and her parents looked in at the door. "The room is reserved for you kiddies, and we can only peep in at the windows."

Dolly and Dotty soon found their friends and crossed the room to join the Shepherd Clan.

Pauline looked very lovely in her elaborate costume, and the boys were really fine as shepherd lads.

As the two girls approached, Pauline whispered to them, with an air of triumph, "You see the caps are plenty big enough!" and sure enough the three boys wore their caps, set jauntily on the side of their heads; but without a doubt the bands were amply large.

"So you see, I did know something after all," Pauline went on, and Dolly said frankly, "You did, Polly; you were right and we were wrong."

Dotty was not quite so smilingly gracious, but she had a strong sense of justice and she said, "They are big enough, Pauline, I was mistaken," and then the dancing began.

There were only simple dances as the children had not mastered the intricacies of modern steps, and there was much fun and gay good-natured banter. The Shepherds and Shepherdesses danced first with each other, but later others joined them and the clan separated.

But the last dance before supper Dolly danced with Carroll Clifton.

At the finish they sat for a moment under some palms to rest, and Carroll took off his cap and held it in his hand.

As a matter of fact, Dolly had forgotten all about the cap discussion, but suddenly her eyes fell on the inside of the cap, as Carroll held it carelessly upside down on his knee.

She could hardly believe her eyes, but she looked again and sure enough, she was right! A full inch of material had been let into the band at the back to make it larger. Dolly stared at it, and then taking the cap, as if to admire it, she said, "I wonder if this is the one I made. You know we girls made the shepherd caps, and I hope you're duly grateful."

"Yes, nice cap-makers you are!" said Carroll, banteringly. "They were so little we couldn't get them on. I told Polly and she gathered them in last night and took them up to her room and made them bigger. I guess she spent half the night doing it, for her light was burning pretty late."

Dolly said nothing, but a wave of indignation swept over her to think Pauline should so deceive her. To think she should be so small and petty as when she found herself in the wrong to secretly rectify her own mistake and then triumphantly announce to the girls that the caps were big enough after all!

Of course they were big enough, after she had set a piece in each one! Dolly smiled to herself to think what an undertaking it must have been, for that alteration, and it was done neatly, meant a troublesome bit of ripping and sewing.

Carroll looked at her inquiringly.

"Well," he said, "is it the one you made? You seem desperately interested in it!"

"I don't know whether it's the one or not. But it doesn't matter, they're all alike. Put it on, Carroll, they're all going out to supper now, and it spoils your costume not to wear it."

Supper was a gay feast. It was the one occasion of the year when the children were allowed in the dining-room at night, and there were snapping-crackers and especial varieties of cakes and ices and jellies suited to juvenile tastes.

After supper the young guests were supposed to say good-night and the party was over.

As they went upstairs, Dolly pulled Dotty back beside her, and at the same moment whispered to Tod to let her take his cap.

Unnoticed by any one else, Dolly showed Dotty the piecing inside, and putting her finger on her lip, shook her head as an admonition to be silent. Then she returned the cap to Tod, who hadn't noticed the incident especially, and on the upper landing of the great staircase, the children said their gay good-nights and went off to their various apartments.

"Now, what do you think of that?" said the fair-haired Shepherdess, not waiting to take off her fancy costume, but pulling the black-haired Shepherdess down to the window-seat beside her.

This was the spot where the girls sat nearly every night to talk over the events of the day. The wide velvet-cushioned seat with its many pillows, was cosy and comfortable, and the view of the ocean and the sound of the rolling waves made these evening chats very happy and confidential.

"But I don't understand," said Dotty, looking puzzled. "You motioned for me not to speak a word, so I didn't. But what does it mean? Who put that piece in Tod's cap, his mother?"

"No; Pauline did it! She sneaked those caps away to her room last night, and sat up till all hours piecing those pieces in. And a sweet job she must have had of it! Why, it's about as much trouble to piece a thing like that, as to make a whole cap!"

"Pauline did it?" still Dotty couldn't understand. "Why, she said this evening that the caps were all right and big enough."

"Of course they were, after she pieced the bands out longer! She did it herself, Dotty, and then pretended to us that they were just as we had left them. At least she meant us to think that, for she said, 'Now don't you see they're all right?' and she didn't tell us she had fixed them."

"How do you know she did it? Maybe Mrs. Brown or Liza did it."

"Carroll told me Polly did it herself. After she went to her room last night. He says her light was burning awful late because she had to fix the three caps."

"The deceitful girl! If that isn't the limit! Just wait till I see her, I'll tell her what I think of her!"

"Now, Dotty, that's just what I don't want you to do. I knew how you'd feel about this thing, and honest, at first I thought I wouldn't tell you, 'cause if I hadn't, you never would have known. But we never do have secrets from each other, and so when I found it out, I thought I ought to tell you. But I don't want you to quarrel with Pauline about it. Won't you let it go, Dot, and never say anything to her on the subject?"

"No, I won't, Dolly. She told a story, or if she didn't tell it right out, she made us think what wasn't true, and it's just the same. She ought to be shown up. Tod and Tad and her own brother, too, ought to know what a mean thing she did. It's only justice, Dolly, that they should. You're so easy-going you'd forgive anything and forget it, too! But I can't. I've got to tell that Clifton girl what I think of her. Oh, I never heard of such meanness! Why Dollyrinda Fayre,—you or I would scorn to do such a thing!"

"Of course we would, Dot, but I don't know as it's up to us to tell Pauline Clifton what she ought to do."

"It isn't that, Dolly; we're not her teachers, and I don't care what she does,—to other people. But she needn't think she can do a thing like that, and act as if we didn't know anything, when we told her she was wrong, and then when she finds she is wrong to go and fix it up on the sly and pretend she was right all along! No-sir-ee! I won't stand for it. I'll show her up in all her meanness and deceit and I'll do it before the boys, too. She ought to be made to feel cheap! The idea!"

Dolly waited in silence until Dotty's wrath had spent itself. She had known Dotty would act like this, but she hoped to calm her justifiable anger.

"Well, all right, Dot," she said at last; "then if you still persist in quarrelling with Pauline about this thing, and if you won't agree not to say anything to her about it, then I'm going to ask you not to, just for my sake. I don't often ask you a favour seriously, Dotty Rose, but

I do now. If you're a friend of mine and if you really care anything about me, won't you promise, just because 'I ask it, not to say anything to Pauline about those caps?"

The two Shepherdesses faced each other in silence. Both were sitting cross-legged in Turkish fashion on the wide divan, and as they had not turned on their room lights, only the moonlight that streamed across the ocean illumined the two earnest faces.

Fair-haired Dolly was pale in her earnestness and her blue eyes looked beseechingly at her friend.

The black-haired Shepherdess was flushed with anger. Her crook had fallen to the floor and she had tossed her hat beside it. Her black eyes snapped and her curly head shook as she refused Dolly's request. But the pleading voice kept on, until at last kindness conquered, and Dotty Rose gave in.

"All right, you dear old thing," she cried, as she grabbed Dolly round the neck, "you've a Heavenly disposition, and I'm a horrid, ugly thing, but I'll do as you say, because you ask me to."

"You're not ugly, Dotty, a bit; only you have a high temper, and your sense of justice makes you feel like getting even with people. And I don't say you're not right. Why, of course there is such a thing as righteous indignation, and this may be the place for it. Only, I do want to have my way this time. You see, we're going home day after to-morrow, and very likely we'll never see the Cliftons again, after we leave here. They don't come here every summer like we do. And I hate to spoil these two last days with a horrid squabble, when we six have been so nice and chummy and pleasant all the time we've been here. You needn't have much to do with Pauline, if you don't want to, but just for two days, can't you just be decently polite to her, and not say anything about this business?"

"I can and I will," said Dotty, heartily; "but you needn't think, old lady, that it's because I'm a meek and mild little lamb, and don't feel like telling that girl what I think of her! No, sir! It's because,— well first because you ask me to; and second, because I'm the guest of you and your people, and it wouldn't be a bit nice of me to stir up an unpleasantness that probably everybody would know about. So, unless Miss Pauline Clifton refers to it herself, she'll never hear of that cap subject from me!"

"You're an old trump, Dotty, and I love you a million bushels! And I'm glad we're going home so soon, and oh, just think! we'll start off to school together, and we'll both go to High School, and we'll have just the same lessons, and we'll be together every day. Dotty Rose, I'm glad I've got you for a friend!"

"You're not half as glad as I am, Dolly Fayre!"

"We'll always be friends, whatever happens, won't we?" said Dolly; "and we'll always tell each other everything."

"Always and always!" said the other Shepherdess, and they sealed their compact with a kiss.

And the big, round-faced moon smiled at them across the night-blue ocean, and tried to make up his mind which of the two D's he was more fond of.

THE END

THE END